BIG SKY SECRETS

AMITY STEFFEN

LOVE INSPIRED SUSPENSE
INSPIRATIONAL ROMANCE

LOVE INSPIRED® SUSPENSE
INSPIRATIONAL ROMANCE

Recycling programs
for this product may
not exist in your area.

ISBN-13: 978-1-335-59759-5

Big Sky Secrets

For questions and comments about the quality of this book, please contact us at CustomerService@Harlequin.com.

Love Inspired
22 Adelaide St. West, 41st Floor
Toronto, Ontario M5H 4E3, Canada
www.LoveInspired.com

Printed in U.S.A.

Thou shalt not be afraid for the terror by night;
nor for the arrow that flieth by day.
—*Psalm* 91:5

To my daughter-in-law Kelli. The first time I met you,
you were barely old enough to drive and you told me
you were going to be a police officer someday.
I'm so proud of you for following your dream.
Thank you for all you do!

"Get down in your seat," he ordered.

This couldn't be happening. Fear and anger sizzled through his body. He was putting Cassie's life at risk *again*.

"Why?" Cassie demanded, though she did as he requested.

He slouched down as well.

"Because I don't know what's up with that truck."

Cassie reached for her purse, which was nestled between her feet. Eric instinctively knew she was reaching for her gun. Before she had a chance to pull it out, the big truck nudged Eric's back bumper.

His tires slid across the slick pavement. A covered bridge with a concrete guardrail loomed up ahead, growing closer by the second. Eric could see the roiling water of the rain soaked river raging below.

"Hold on!" he growled.

Cassie braced her hands against the dashboard.

The truck plowed into them again, this time shoving them toward the steep incline right before the bridge.

Faster than he could blink, his old vehicle was careening down the hill, racing toward the swollen, churning water...

Amity Steffen lives in northern Minnesota with her two boys and two spoiled cats. She's a voracious reader and a novice baker. She enjoys watching her sons play baseball in the summer and would rather stay indoors in the winter. She's worked in the education field for more years than she cares to count, but writing has always been her passion. Amity loves connecting with readers, so please visit her at Facebook.com/amitysteffenauthor.

Books by Amity Steffen

Love Inspired Suspense

Reunion on the Run
Colorado Ambush
Big Sky Secrets

Visit the Author Profile page at LoveInspired.com.

ONE

Eric Montgomery glanced in the rearview mirror of his double-cab truck. The reflection staring back at him made his heart kick in his chest. Dark brown eyes, identical to his own, locked on to his. The kid had a mop of nearly black hair, also matching his. The child's expression was full of woe.

Eric looked back at the road as the windshield wipers methodically whisked away the heavy barrage of rain. He gripped the steering wheel, willing his vehicle to stay on the blacktop and not hydroplane into the ditch. It wasn't a great time to be out, but he had an errand to run that couldn't be put off a day longer.

"I want my mom," Wyatt said mournfully, possibly for the thousandth time.

"I know," he said gently to the child, his *son*. The son he only a few days ago found out existed. He took a deep breath, tried to tamp down the frustration he felt, the anger at having been deprived of three whole years. "We're going to visit someone who can hopefully help us find her."

Wyatt frowned and Eric's heart sank. So far, nothing he had done seemed to please the child Eric didn't blame Wyatt for his obstinance.

Lorelei Coffman, a woman whom he'd dated four years ago, a woman who had walked out of his life without even a goodbye, had shown up at his ranch the other day. Her parting gift back then had been to wipe out his bank account. And to keep his son from him.

Until now.

What kind of woman did that?

The same kind of woman who barged into his home with three-year-old Wyatt on her hip and a small suitcase dangling from her fist. Eric had nearly fallen over from disbelief when she said the boy was his.

Then again, Wyatt was Eric's mini-me if ever there was one. Before he had time to question her, she'd claimed nausea, had pressed her hand to her stomach and had, indeed, looked convincingly ill. She had asked to use his bathroom. When she didn't emerge after five minutes, he went to demand answers. The window was open, the screen popped out and the traitorous woman gone.

He wasn't even all that shocked.

Scrawled on the mirror in her signature crimson lipstick was the cryptic message—*Keep him safe.*

Eric glanced in the rearview mirror again, this time not concentrating on the passenger in the back seat. The storm clouds were thick, heavy, darkening the sky. It was easy to spot the headlights behind him again. He had seen them a few miles back and hadn't thought it too unusual that someone else was heading into town. What was strange was that they had been steadily closing the distance. In this weather, that was hardly wise, but some people were reckless.

Still, those words scrawled in red caused paranoia to shimmy down his spine. Dread spilled into his stomach, spreading into his limbs, causing his already tight grip on the steering wheel to become tighter still.

Keep him safe.

Safe from what? He didn't know. From *something*? From *someone*? If so, who? Or had she just been generalizing? Not likely. How was he supposed to keep Wyatt safe when she had disappeared without having the decency to clue him in? His frustration grew, seemed to sizzle. Eric had made a lot of bad choices in the year after Ella, his twin, died. His life had felt as if it were spiraling out of control. He'd felt lost, had strayed from his faith, and it had taken him a few years to set himself straight again. His relationship with Lorelei was something he now regretted. But not Wyatt. He wasn't sure how it was possible, but he already loved the little guy.

He would keep him safe. Or die trying. In all the upheaval and confusion of the past few days, that was something he did know.

Lightning forked across the sky a split second before a ferocious clap of thunder shook the vehicle. Wyatt whimpered in the back seat. Eric's heart went out to the child. Everything had to be so overwhelming for him.

The address Eric had memorized this afternoon was only a mile or so away. The office was on the edge of the small town of Mulberry Creek. He'd found it online, thought about simply calling, but had worried that the proprietor would be too busy, would maybe even refuse to see him. Or put him off. But he couldn't be put off. He needed help. Now. Yesterday would've been even better. He wasn't going to take any chances of being turned away.

No, this meeting had to take place in person. He would plead, offer to pay double, whatever it took to find the woman who had betrayed him one time too many. For his son's sake, he needed to find her because they both deserved some answers.

Entering the town, he navigated his truck down the rain-soaked street, found a parking spot on the curb of a nondescript gray storefront. C. J. Anderson, Private Investigator. The white vinyl moniker, fairly discreet, clung to the window, announcing he'd arrived at the right place.

He glanced behind him, looking for the vehicle he'd thought might be following him, but saw nothing. There were few other cars out on this stormy afternoon. He shut off his truck and stepped onto the slick asphalt.

The sound of a gunshot boomed through the quiet as a dark SUV barreled toward him, seemingly from nowhere. Eric's door was still open, and the bullet tore through the window, shattering it. Instinctively, Eric ducked and scrambled to get to the other side of the truck. Squatting, squinting against the pelting rain, he ran around the front of the vehicle.

All he could think of was Wyatt buckled into the back seat, strapped to the car seat Lorelei had apparently left on his porch before taking off again. He had just found out about his son, and he was *not* about to lose him.

Two more gunshots ripped through the air. He could hear the bullets tearing through his vehicle, probably the fender, though he didn't care. He hurled himself toward the back passenger door, nearly ripping it off the hinges to get to the precious cargo inside.

Cassie Anderson bolted from her desk the moment she heard gunshots. For just a split second she had thought it was thunder, but then the sound registered for what it was. Her attention flew to the man parked right outside the large window overlooking the street. He had his back to her, but his movements seemed frantic. Her heart stuttered when she realized he was scrambling to pull a child from the back seat.

Were they the targets?

Instead of ducking for cover, she ran to the front door and flung it open just as the man pivoted with a small child in his arms. Her heart catapulted in her chest, surprise rippling through her when she realized who it was.

"Eric," she called, "in here."

He darted toward her as conflicting emotions skittered across his face. Shock. Disbelief. Despite showing up at her office, he clearly had not been expecting *her*.

Oh, yes, she could relate. Eric Montgomery was just about the last man on earth she'd ever expect to seek her out, on purpose or not. The last time they had spoken, it had not ended well. He had been furious with her, and to say he had shattered her heart would be an understatement.

It was a testament to his desperation that he didn't hesitate.

The moment he crossed her threshold, she shoved the door closed and flipped the dead bolt into place. A moment later a man dressed in black, face obscured by the hood pulled over his head, darted down the sidewalk and stopped in front of the door, gun raised. Cassie shoved Eric and the child toward the back of the building even as the glass-windowed door shattered, sending bits of glass flying.

The child screamed.

Cassie's heart raced as she glanced over her shoulder. The man was trying to lean in to turn the lock on the door but couldn't quite reach. She allowed herself only an instant to assess his struggle as she urged Eric toward the storage room.

"Where can we go?" Eric demanded, holding the child to his chest, shielding him with his body even as he ran, looking for cover.

"Go straight," Cassie ordered. "The door leads to the alley."

They darted through her storeroom. She grabbed her purse off the hook as they hustled past, not taking time to nab her coat, and only moments later they were racing out the door and down the dank, rutted alley.

The moment they burst from the building, icy rain pelted her body, drenching her. Their feet pounded against the gravel.

Cassie registered the sound of sirens wailing in the distance and knew someone must have called in the disturbance.

The child sobbed.

The frigid spring rain stabbed through her knitted sweater, biting at her skin. The discomfort was nothing compared to her fear. Had the man gotten into her office? Were they already in his sights? Would a bullet rip through her spine at any second?

What about Eric? What about the child?

They were all in danger, and she needed to get them to safety.

"Run to the end of the block," she ordered, keeping pace with Eric, "then take a left. My Jeep Cherokee is in the municipal parking lot across the street."

Cassie dared a glance over her shoulder, her feet skidding around beneath her as the brick buildings seemed to close in on them. They had no choice now but to race straight ahead. Especially because the gunman came into view, bursting out of her office and charging after them.

His gunshot echoed, reverberating in her bones as something hot and painful tore across the side of her head. She shrieked as pain seared over her, blurring her vision for just a moment.

Eric whirled, his arms protectively encasing the child.

"Cassie!" His voice was frantic, his eyes shocked. "Go!"

Seeing she was upright seemed to be all the encouragement he needed. He took off again.

She realized then that they may not make it to the end of the block. She pulled her Ruger from her purse, spun and fired at the alley, near the man's feet. He dived behind a dumpster, and she took off after Eric.

As they finally cleared the alley and rounded the brick building, she pressed herself against the cold, rough surface and peeked around the corner, taking aim once more. She spotted the man as he raced back the way he'd come.

Perfect. She realized she'd scared him off by firing back. Yet that didn't mean they were out of danger. Not yet. Not standing out here, in the open, on the sidewalk.

What if the man hadn't been alone?

"This way?" Eric asked, already on the move. He nodded toward the parking lot she'd mentioned.

"Yes." She tugged her keys from her purse, hit the button for remote start, an essential luxury during the brutally cold Montana winters, and clicked another button to unlock the doors.

They raced to her silver Cherokee, the only vehicle running in the lot.

While Eric hopped in back, buckling up the child, she hustled into the driver's seat. Her head throbbed, and she blinked hard to regain her vision as the wipers cleared the windshield.

"Cassie?" Eric's voice was full of alarm. "Were you hit?"

She slid a quick glance over her shoulder. He looked horrified, but that didn't stop her from doing what she knew needed to be done. She whipped around and, as quickly as she dared, maneuvered through the lot. As she drove, she gingerly touched the back of her head with her fingers. They came away smeared with blood.

"Yes, I was hit." She winced. "I mean, no. Not by a bullet. I think his shot hit the brick wall, and I was hit by debris."

Eric groaned. "I'm so sorry. I don't know what's going on. I—" He interrupted himself to shout, "Watch out!"

She slammed on the brakes. The Cherokee jolted to a halt a moment before emerging from the lot and onto the city street. A black SUV had raced around the corner. It roared past. Cassie caught a glimpse of a man in the passenger seat. The hood that had obscured his face now rested around his neck. He was mostly a blur driving by through the rain, but she caught sight of a bald head. White, chubby cheeks. In that instant, he reminded her of a cue ball. Apparently he caught sight of her as well. The SUV screeched to a halt, fishtailing a bit on the drenched road.

Cassie yanked the steering wheel to the left and took off out of the lot in the opposite direction. The SUV attempted a U-turn in the middle of the street, but the maneuver was difficult due to cars parked on either side of the road.

She took advantage of the precious seconds that were granted to her, grateful that, due to the inclement weather, there were few other people out right now. She rolled through the first intersection, cruised down the street and rolled through a second intersection as she headed toward the police station.

"Here they come." Eric had twisted around in his seat to look out the window. "They're coming fast."

Before she reached the third intersection, the SUV recklessly closed the distance between them.

She carefully drove through, grateful for the lack of traffic, and before she reached the fourth, she let out a gasp of horror as her rearview mirror showed the SUV barreling through the intersection she'd just cleared. It plowed into a squad car with its lights flashing. She assumed the officer was on the way to her office, the scene of the shooting.

Eric let out a pained groan as she slowed. "That was a hard hit, but at least the SUV hit the passenger door."

"Do we go back to help?" What if the officer was hurt? But the men in the SUV had guns, so would trying to help be wise? Or would they just get in the way? Put themselves and the officer at risk?

"I think everyone's okay," Eric replied.

A glance over her shoulder confirmed he was probably right. She caught a glimpse of the SUV as it tore away from the crash site, taking a side street. A split second later, the police cruiser whipped around and gave chase.

Cassie blew out a sigh of relief, equally grateful that

no one appeared to be seriously injured and the SUV was no longer on their tail.

"That was too close," Eric said.

Cassie silently agreed. If the SUV hadn't slammed into the cruiser, it would likely be slamming into her rear bumper right now. She pushed the thought away because the repercussions of that were too terrible to comprehend.

"We're almost to the police station." She pointed out the obvious in an effort to soothe her own nerves.

Thank You, Lord, for keeping us safe.

Cassie spotted another cruiser on the cross street, hurrying along with lights flashing, and suspected there were several en route to her office a block away.

"I think that's the safest place for you two right now." If only she could get them there without incident.

"I won't argue with that," Eric muttered. "I don't know what's going on, but I'm sorry I pulled you into this mess. Thank you for having our back in the alley. When did you start carrying a gun?"

He sounded equal parts impressed and stunned.

"When I became a PI and started getting into sticky situations," she replied.

"Have you had to use it often?"

"Only at the shooting range," she admitted, then decided it was her turn to ask the questions. "I know you said you don't know what's going on. So why were you coming to see me?"

"I didn't know it was *you*."

His answer didn't surprise her, so she tried not to feel hurt by the response.

Whether he had meant to or not, Eric *had* come to

her. No one came to her office unless they needed assistance in one form or another.

Her guilt over what had happened in the past weighed heavily on her. She was sure his anger at her still burned deep. If she could help him now, she would.

"I'm sorry about your office window," he said, his tone resigned. "But I'm grateful you were there."

"It's okay, Eric. I'm glad I was able to help." She meant it.

"Daddy, I'm scared," the child whimpered.

Daddy? It shouldn't have come as a surprise, and on some level, it did not, because the child looked just like him. Still, she'd had no idea that Eric Montgomery had a son. Certainly not a son as old as this child was. In the chaos, she hadn't had time to work through that obvious detail.

Judging by the bewildered look on Eric's face as she glanced at him in the mirror, she realized she wasn't the only one stunned by this fact.

Daddy.

Wyatt had just called him Daddy. The word seemed to reverberate through his brain. When Lorelei had introduced them, she had said, "Eric, this is Wyatt. Wyatt, this is your daddy." The child had eyed him warily but hadn't replied. He hadn't said much of anything, other than that he wanted his mom, since the moment she had disappeared.

"Don't be scared, Wyatt," Eric soothed. He wrapped an arm around his thin shoulders, his heart cracking a little when he realized how badly Wyatt was shaking. "I won't let anything happen to you. It'll be okay."

It would be, he vowed. He didn't know what Lorelei had gotten them into, but he was determined to get them out of it. His anger at her flared all over again. What she had done to *him* years ago, that was one thing. But whatever she was involved in now had clearly put his son in danger. That made him furious.

Obviously she had known, because she had warned him.

But needing to keep him safe from a gunman? Eric wondered bitterly. Where had Lorelei been all this time? Where in the world had she run off to the other night? Although perhaps he shouldn't be surprised. Disappearing seemed to be what she did best.

Why were they after *him* now? Were they hoping he could lead them to her? That would be awfully hard to do if he was dead. Were they after Wyatt? But why?

His stomach lurched when he realized the danger he had put Cassie in. Knowing Wyatt was at risk was bad enough, but now he had two people to worry about.

"You were coming to see me?" Cassie pressed ahead with the question he thought he'd avoided.

"I was looking for C. J. Anderson," he corrected. Then winced. "You're C.J., aren't you." It wasn't a question. He'd known Cassie most of his life. Knew her last name was Anderson, but it was such a common last name that it hadn't occurred to him that C.J. and Cassie were one and the same.

"Yes. Cassie Jolie," she replied. "Even in this day and age I realized early on that some people are still a bit biased. I found it helped if they got to know me before forming an opinion as to whether or not I, as a female, am a competent investigator."

"Are you?" he demanded. "Competent?" He heard

the challenge in his words but didn't care. Now more than ever he needed to find Wyatt's mother.

"I have a list of satisfied clients who would say so," she shot back.

He gritted his teeth. Had he known C.J. was short for Cassie Jolie, he never would've even considered hiring her. It had nothing to do with the fact that she was female and everything to do with the fact that his sister Ella might still be alive if it weren't for Cassie.

No. That was in the past. He had to stop thinking that way. Deep in his heart, he knew Cassie wasn't to blame.

She diverted her gaze from the mirror, and without either of them having to say anything, it was clear she knew exactly where his thoughts had gone. She was no longer the ponytail-wearing, gum-snapping pest he remembered from his youth, no longer his sister's very best friend.

This was the woman he'd railed at in the hospital parking lot a half dozen years ago. He had told her that day that he hoped to never see her face again. And he'd meant it, his grief over losing Ella so deep he could barely stand it. He knew now that he'd been lashing out, that Cassie hadn't deserved the entirety of his wrath. Though he still, after all these years, couldn't help but wonder if Ella would be alive had Cassie handled things differently.

"Care to tell me why you're looking for a PI?" The question tugged him from the awful memory.

"Nope," he bluntly replied. Maybe he owed her an explanation. But he couldn't even begin to explain what had happened. Besides, he'd already caused her enough trouble. Her office was damaged, and she had a gash on her head. Cutting her out as soon as possible was for the best.

It would be for her own safety.

Surely there were other private investigators in town. Ones who wouldn't stir up a whirlwind of old memories and complex emotions. He'd blamed Cassie for Ella's death…but he'd also fancied himself in love with her once, before Ella's illness sent their lives spinning in a direction he'd never wanted to go.

Oh, best not to let his thoughts wander that path.

"I'll pull up to the door. You take Wyatt inside. I'll find a parking spot and be right behind you."

He didn't like the idea of leaving her in the parking lot alone. He'd meant it when he'd said that he didn't know anything about the people who were after him. Was it just the pair in the black SUV? Or were there others?

"Park right in front of the building," Eric said. "We'll go in together. I'm pretty sure they aren't going to hassle you about not taking a parking spot under the circumstances."

She apparently agreed, because she pulled up to the police station as close as possible, forgoing a spot in the lot.

Cutting the engine, she asked, "Ready?"

He didn't miss the way her gaze scanned the street or the fact that she'd retrieved her weapon once more.

"Let's get inside," Cassie ordered. "We can sort the rest out later."

Eric agreed and reached over for Wyatt. He could hardly believe his eyes when he realized the kiddo was asleep. How was that even possible after the recent excitement? Wyatt had hardly slept the past few nights and had spent the day on the verge of tears, so maybe he was crashing after an adrenaline rush.

As he scooped his son into his arms, he wondered if three-year-olds typically took naps. He had no idea. Should he have tried to make him take one this afternoon? Well, he hadn't, and the boy was clearly exhausted. He felt woefully inept at being a father. The fact that it wasn't his fault that he didn't know his son did little to soothe his guilt over not knowing the first thing about parenting.

"A car's coming," Cassie warned, her tone clearly implying it could be a threat.

Eric glanced over his shoulder and spotted the headlights. The vehicle—he couldn't tell from this distance what make it was—seemed to be slowly rolling toward them. Was it just someone on their way home from work? Or was it someone who wouldn't think twice about putting a bullet through him? He didn't stop to think it over as he hustled down the sidewalk. Wyatt's head rested on his shoulder, bobbing with every hurried step Eric took.

He was hyperaware of his surroundings. Acutely mindful that Cassie was behind him.

He reached the door, shoved it open and surged through it. Instead of feeling grateful, hopeful that they'd reached a place of safety, he had a foreboding sense that this nightmare was not over.

His instincts told him it had only just begun.

TWO

Cassie leaned back in her chair, trying not to shiver in the chilly room. Her clothes were damp, and there was nothing she could do about it. Instead, she was almost afraid to breathe for fear that Eric would remember that she was there, right beside him at the interview table.

Officer Hughes, a rookie who had come out to greet them, had administered first aid to the wound on Cassie's head. She'd cleaned up the gash, added antibiotic, then handed her an ice pack. She'd announced she didn't think stitches were necessary but encouraged Cassie to be checked out by a doctor all the same, citing a concussion as a possibility.

Cassie had declined a doctor but had accepted a few painkillers. She'd used the ice pack just briefly but placed it on the table as the conversation picked up.

Already they had learned that the officer who had given chase to the SUV had lost the vehicle. Once they reached the highway, the damage to the cruiser from the crash, and the inclement weather, had made a chase unsafe. The officer had been unwilling to put innocent lives in danger and, subsequently, had to allow the SUV to speed away.

Cassie also knew that a team was in her office, collecting evidence, though other than a few bullets, it was unlikely the perp had left anything behind.

Now that her head wasn't quite as fuzzy, she was zeroed in on Eric's conversation with the detective. She listened intently as he cradled his sleeping son on his lap, recalling earlier events, those that she had missed.

The biggest bit of info that she gleaned was that his ex had shown up with a son he didn't know existed.

Cassie could only imagine what a blow that was to someone as family oriented as Eric. Missing three years of his son's life, he had to be crushed. Or furious. Probably a bit of both.

After Lorelei had disappeared once again, he'd called the police. Due to the circumstances, they hadn't considered her a missing person.

"I got the impression her disappearance the other night wasn't taken seriously," Eric said.

"Despite the fact that she had a history of running, that there was only one set of footprints in the mud, leading to tire tracks that were likely her vehicle, I did have the department on the lookout," Detective Mateo Bianchi said. "I didn't like the message on the mirror. That struck me as worrisome. Mothers don't typically drop their children off with someone the child doesn't know, then take off. Not saying it doesn't happen, but it just didn't sit right with me."

"Have you found anything?" Eric demanded.

Cassie wondered that as well. She was taking in every word they were saying, filing it away, knowing she would go over the entire conversation again later, once she'd heard all there was to hear.

The detective shook his head. "No one has seen her.

However, the fact that you were shot at today, that changes things." He cut his gaze to Cassie, then back to Eric. "Am I correct to assume that you planned on hiring Ms. Anderson?"

"That would be correct." Eric flicked a quick glance at her. Cassie couldn't tell by that look if he was still planning on hiring her, now that he knew who she was. "It's nothing against the department. It's just that I know you have plenty of other cases to keep you busy. I thought it wouldn't hurt to have someone else looking into it. I had some information. It wasn't much, but I wrote down all the details about Lorelei that I could remember. You know, birthday, where she grew up, that sort of thing. I was hoping to hand it over to a private investigator." He frowned. "I left that information in my truck."

The truck that had been shot up and was now on the way to be impounded.

"Can it be duplicated?" Cassie spoke up for the first time. The thought that he had a file for her to investigate, information for her to dig into, had her pulse racing and her mind whirling. She loved her job, loved research, loved the sense of accomplishment when she finally solved her clients' life puzzles.

"It can be duplicated." Eric frowned, though, and Cassie had a hunch that just because it could be replicated didn't mean he was going to share it with her. He had, after all, thought he was meeting with a stranger.

She bit back her disappointment.

"I'd like a copy," the detective said. "Right now, we don't have much to go on."

"Sure."

"Are you sure the child is yours?" he continued. "I mean, he looks like you, but—"

"He's mine," Eric interrupted, an edge to his tone. "There was a copy of his birth certificate in the suitcase Lorelei left behind. He was born in Billings, only a few hours from here. I'm not listed as the father—no one is—but the timing fits. Apparently she was pregnant when she left town around four years ago." His tone was full of frustration. "I don't know why she took my son from me, but I have no doubt he is *my* son. Regardless, I had my doctor run a DNA test yesterday morning. Not really for my peace of mind, but in case any legal issues come up. It'll take a few days for the results to come in, but I want my name added to the birth certificate as soon as possible. No one is ever going to take him away from me. Not again."

Cassie's heart swelled, impressed by the level of love Eric clearly already felt for his child.

"That's a good plan," Detective Bianchi said. "As soon as paternity is established, you'll want to submit the appropriate paperwork to the vital statistics services. You'll find their office in the courthouse. They'll assist you in getting everything squared away. I suggest you take care of that as soon as you are able."

"I will, sir, thank you."

"Ms. Anderson." Detective Bianchi turned his attention to her. "I've heard Mr. Montgomery's version of events. Now I'd like to hear yours."

Eric couldn't stop the wave of guilt that crashed over him as he listened to Cassie describe seeing him pull up, being shot at, then their race out of her office, essentially running for their lives. He admired how cool and calm she sounded. Did that come from being a private investigator? Did she find herself in these types of predicaments often? He highly doubted it, causing him to admire her even more. She handled the situation like a pro, though he suspected being shot at was entirely new for her.

He inwardly groaned. She was shot at because of *him*. Years ago, he had blamed her for Ella's death, and now here he was, almost getting *her* killed. The irony was not lost on him. When he thought of that night, he was filled with shame. He wouldn't be surprised if Cassie hated him. He kind of hated himself for some of the things he'd said.

Yet Cassie was here, trying to help him out. He admired her all the more for it.

"You never saw his face?"

"Not clearly," Cassie replied. "His head was covered when he was in front of my office. Then later, when they drove by, rain was streaming down the windshield. I got the impression he was bald. His cheeks were chubby, bare of stubble." She grimaced. "It's not a professional opinion, but he seemed white and pasty and vaguely reminded me of a cue ball."

"Could you pick him out in a lineup?" he asked.

"No, I don't think so," Cassie said, her tone full of disappointment. "Because of the storm, my view of him was simply not good. I couldn't make out his features. I only had an overall, general impression."

"Can you think of anything else that might be helpful? Any detail, no matter how small?" the detective pressed.

Cassie's brow furrowed, as if thinking hard.

"I heard the gunshots, and then everything happened so fast. I was focused on Eric, though I didn't realize it was him at first, getting a child out of the truck. I let Eric in, and the next thing I knew, a man dressed in black ran up to the window, and we were being shot at."

Her gaze slid to his, locking on him for a moment, and a haunted expression flashed across her face. Was she thinking about how he had almost gotten her killed? A feeling of remorse assaulted him.

"I'm sorry," he said automatically. "I never meant to... I mean, if I'd known—"

She shook her head. "No, there's something else."

The detective hitched a brow as Cassie turned her attention back to him.

"There was a moment when Eric had his back to the window as the gunman ran up. The guy could have shot Eric, square in the back. It was dark and gloomy outside, because of the storm, and the lights were on in my office. He would've had a clear view, a perfect shot. Either he was a *terrible* shot, or he didn't actually want to hit Eric."

Trepidation buzzed up his spine, causing it to tingle with dread, knowing he'd been in the sights of a gunman at close range. The man could've taken him out.

He could be dead right now.

Why wasn't he?

She glanced at him and winced. "Actually, I wonder if he was afraid of hitting Wyatt. It's the only reason I can think of that he wouldn't have taken you out when he had the chance."

All the air whooshed out of his lungs.

Eric glanced down at his sleeping son. Had his life been spared because of Wyatt? Ironic, since Eric suspected that his son, in some roundabout way, may be the reason they were being chased.

"Maybe the guy had a conscience and didn't want to hit a child," Detective Bianchi said.

Keep him safe.

"Or maybe he wants Wyatt." A sense of foreboding flooded through Eric as the thought took hold. Was that what Lorelei had meant? He shifted Wyatt gently, unable to keep himself from holding his child a little closer.

Eric was knocked almost senseless by the love he felt for this boy. How was it possible to love someone so much after just meeting them?

"Maybe," the detective said, his tone noncommittal as he scribbled down more notes.

Eric glanced at Cassie. A worry line was etched between her pale green eyes. Despite their past, he knew she was a good person, and her concern over Wyatt made him feel as if he wasn't entirely alone in this.

"Tell me again how long you dated this woman."

"About six months," Eric said.

"Was it serious?"

"Apparently not," Eric scoffed, "given how she up and left one day. Took a good chunk of my money, too. I stupidly kept my passwords in my desk drawer, and she helped herself to my bank account."

"Did you file a report?"

Eric frowned. "No. I didn't think I could prove it was her." He'd also been embarrassed by his own gullibility. Now he didn't mind so much. Maybe she'd used the money to care for Wyatt. In retrospect, she probably had, and he sincerely wished he'd been able to do more.

Detective Bianchi studied Eric's face. "Any chance she was running from something back then, too?"

That gave Eric pause. Four years ago felt like such a long time. His head had been in such a bad place. His memories—memories he'd decided were best to bury—were hazy now that he was taking them out and dusting them off.

"I guess it's possible. I mean, it never crossed my mind at the time." He cleared his throat. "My younger sister, my twin, had just died. Cancer. I'm the first to admit I was kind of wrapped up in myself. In my grief. I probably missed a lot of signs."

"What about her family? Did you ever meet any of them?"

Eric shook his head. "Lorelei said they died in a car accident when she was seven. She grew up in foster care and didn't have any siblings. I got the impression she didn't have anyone, but she didn't like to talk about it. I tried to be respectful of that, so I never pushed the matter."

"Maybe she simply didn't want you asking about her past," Cassie said quietly.

Eric said nothing but realized Cassie was probably right about that.

"Any chance you'd consider leaving town?" the detective asked. "For your own safety."

"And go where?" Eric wondered. "For how long? Big Sky Ranch isn't going to run itself. Help is hard to find, and it's not like ranchers get vacation time. Besides, even though he's not completely settled, I don't want to uproot Wyatt any more than I have to. My brother, Seth, is an ex-marine. We run the ranch together. He lives on the other side of the property. He's on a business trip, checking out some bulls, but should be home tomorrow. My parents are on vacation, but they live on-site, too."

What rotten timing. His family rarely went any-where. Ranch life made it difficult to up and leave. But his parents had planned their trip ages ago. Then Seth found a bull that he thought was perfect for their program. Eric hadn't thought much of handling the ranch on his own for a few days. Calving season was over, and they'd already moved the cows to the west-ern pasture to graze freely.

"I'll have an officer keep an eye on your ranch to-night," Detective Bianchi said. "The entire force will be on the lookout for the black SUV."

"What about Cassie?"

She waved off Eric's concern. "I live in town, just a few blocks from the station."

"Give me your address and I'll make sure to have someone drive by periodically." Detective Bianchi jot-ted it down as she rattled it off, then turned to Eric. "I'll make sure everyone is on the lookout for Lorelei as well. Do you happen to have a photo?"

"It's an older one, but yes. It's part of the file I com-piled. I'll get it to you."

"I'll send it out to the force," the detective said.

"I'd appreciate that." Eric was grateful for the detec-tive's plan of action but doubted he'd get much sleep tonight, regardless.

"I think we can wrap this up." He flipped the note-book closed. "If either of you think of anything else, please let me know. I'll give you my business card be-fore you go. If I hear anything, I know where to find—"

A sharp knock on the interview room door cut the detective off midsentence. He frowned. "Excuse me a moment. This must be important or they wouldn't in-terrupt." He rose from his seat and exited the room.

Eric strained to hear what was being said on the other side of the door, suspecting it had something to do with him, but the voices were too muffled to make out.

Cassie apparently agreed, because after a moment, she turned from the door and drilled him with her riveting green gaze.

It was disconcerting, being in the same room with her again after all these years, and under such stressful circumstances. But she was all business.

"Eric, you have to give me that file," she stated, her tone brusque.

"No, I don't," he argued, knowing what he should do was put some distance between them. For both their sakes. Otherwise, their emotional states may be as precarious as their physical well-being was at the moment.

Cassie, apparently, didn't see it that way.

"Please," she pressed. "You clearly need help with this. You said yourself that the department isn't going to be able to dedicate ample time to this. Sure, after tonight it'll be more of a priority, but we both know they don't have the resources to devote the time that's needed."

She had a point, and he knew it.

"I don't want to put you in any more danger," he admitted, though that was only part of it. He could still hear the shot of gunfire as it echoed through the alley. Could still hear Cassie's shriek of pain, feel the moment of utter dread when he'd thought—for just a second—she'd been hit. Actually, she *had* been hit, and he could still see the blood streaking her short blond hair. It had been close. Way too close. It could have been a bullet instead of a brick.

She shrugged, but he knew she wasn't nearly as nonchalant as she was trying to appear. "They broke into my office. They know who I am. I'm probably already in danger."

That did *not* make him feel at all better.

"So you see, it's in my best interest to figure this out. The faster we uncover what's going on, the faster we'll *all* be safe."

He wanted to argue with her, but everything she said was so logical.

"You could hire another PI, but no one would work this case as hard as I would," she continued.

"I can't believe you want to help me." *Not after the way I treated you.*

Her gaze flickered to Wyatt, then back to him.

"I want to do it for Ella. I know you think I failed her. I guess I want to make up for that. Wyatt's her nephew. She would want me to do this," she said, her tone passionate. "I know she would've been so excited about becoming an aunt and would've loved him instantly, just like you did."

Yes, he'd loved Wyatt instantly. Was it that obvious? Or since they had grown up together, did Cassie simply know him that well?

She leaned forward and gently wiped a sweaty lock of Wyatt's hair off his forehead, brushing it to the side. Eric felt his heart give a little tug. He wasn't sure if it was because Cassie had mentioned Ella or if it was because she seemed to truly care about Wyatt, though she'd only just met him.

She locked eyes with his. "Please let me do this."

"All right." He carefully pulled his cell phone out of his pocket and tried not to jostle his son. "The file I was bringing to you, it wasn't much. Just some notes I started writing down. I don't have anything concrete. I don't know if you'll be able to do much with the information. There are a few pictures of her, of us together. Not many, just three selfies. She hated having her picture taken." He grimaced. "I thought she was shy. Now I'm wondering if there was more to that."

With a few taps on his phone, he pulled up the file he'd stored. Cassie gave him her contact information, and he sent the file off, not allowing himself time to second-guess the decision.

The truth was, he did need help. And she was right. She had a personal stake in this, both because of her connection to his family and because she had been shot at, too. He knew she'd work hard at digging up some answers.

The door creaked open, and Detective Bianchi strode back into the room, wearing a grim expression. Eric's heart clenched in his chest. He gripped Wyatt a little tighter, taking some comfort in the weight of his son resting against him.

Eric knew, before the detective said the words, that his world was about to shift in a monumental way.

Detective Bianchi lowered himself into the chair and cleared his throat. "A woman's body was pulled from the river a little over an hour ago."

Cassie let out a moan.

Eric said nothing. He felt frozen, dreading the next few moments, wishing them not to come, but unable to stop what he knew he was about to hear.

"We have reason to believe it's Lorelei," the detective continued, his tone soft, yet firm. "There was no ID on her, but the description matches. We need you to identify the body."

Identify the body. They were words no one should ever have to hear. It was a task no one should ever have to face.

Eric sucked in a breath. Scraped a hand through his hair. Glanced down at his sleeping son. Anxiety scurried down his spine, settling in the pit of his stomach, making him feel ill with dread.

As angry as he'd been at Lorelei, he didn't want this. Didn't want his child to grow up without a mother.

"I can have Officer Hughes stay with Wyatt," the detective continued. "She hasn't gone out yet, and several other officers are still downtown at your office."

"I'll stay with Wyatt." Cassie's tone was soft, determined. Comforting.

He met her gaze.

"I'll stay with Wyatt," she said again, her expression filled with compassion. "If he wakes up, at least I'm a familiar face."

It may have been a bit of an overstatement, but she would be more familiar to him than Officer Hughes. And to be honest, he was relieved Cassie had offered to stay. The thought of leaving his son with a stranger, even if she was an officer, was disconcerting. Despite their rocky past, he trusted Cassie.

"Okay," he said, his voice gravelly, his body numb. "I'll do it. I'll identify the body."

Regardless of the late hour, Cassie couldn't sleep. Her mind wouldn't slow down. Anytime she closed her eyes for even a second, she couldn't stop picturing the stoic look on Eric's face when he'd returned to the station and scooped his son into his arms. He didn't have to say a word to her. His demeanor confirmed the body pulled from the river was Lorelei.

Wyatt had been oblivious to the whole ordeal, snoozing on a cot Officer Hughes had scrounged up from somewhere.

Cassie's heart ached for the child. His whole world had gone topsy-turvy with no end in sight.

Her own world felt completely off-kilter as well. Never had she imagined Eric barreling back into her life the way he had. Being twins, he and Ella had been as close as two siblings could be. He'd taken her death harder than Seth and Nina, their younger brother and sister, had. Cassie knew Ella's death had gutted Eric.

She knew he'd been devastated the night Ella slipped from this world, but Cassie had been hurting, too. She and Ella had been best friends since kindergarten. They were two peas in a pod, their mothers always said. They'd gone through so many firsts together. Everything from losing baby teeth to suffering through their first unrequited crushes.

The night Ella had died, Eric had lashed out at her, said things that were hurtful and untrue. He had shattered her already battered heart. In a perfect world, they would have leaned on each other, shared each other's pain. Instead, they hadn't spoken since, and Cassie thought maybe that was for the best.

At one time she had cared deeply for him. Not that it mattered. Nothing had ever come of her feelings. Not really.

She'd help Eric out, but then move on, leaving him in the past, which was exactly where he belonged. She would not allow her heart to try to resurrect the feelings she'd once had for him, would not dwell on the single, perfect kiss they had shared. There was no point, other than to cause herself more pain and heartache.

There'd already been plenty of that in her lifetime.

No. She was not going to reminisce about Eric. Or think about his adorable surprise of a son. She just wasn't going to do it.

Instead, she was going to treat this case like any other case—examine the problem, remain professional and do what was possible to solve this mystery. The sooner the better. For more reasons than she could count.

Knowing sleep wouldn't come easily, and unable to help herself, Cassie had turned on her laptop and dug into the file Eric had sent her the moment she'd returned home.

Lorelei Rose Coffman was from Goodrich, Wisconsin. Aged twenty-six with blue eyes and brunette hair. Cassie was sure she'd found a match. Only, well, it was complicated.

Her heart beat out a staccato rhythm as she stared at her computer screen. The information she had pulled up on the woman could not be refuted. She had checked, double-checked, looked into multiple resources. There was simply no way she was wrong.

Finding out Lorelei was dead had been a blow to Eric. But what Cassie had just discovered was going to rock the foundation of his life to the very core.

THREE

Cassie shivered against the chilly morning air as she hustled up Eric's front steps clutching a folder and her laptop to her chest. The morning was overcast, but so far, more rain had stayed at bay. Her light footsteps tapped against the porch that wrapped around the log-sided ranch house. She had spent a lot of time here in her youth, back when this was the family home. Once Eric's father, James, had decided to give up ranching, he and his wife, Julia, had renovated the bunkhouse down the hill into their retirement home. Now Seth and Eric ran the ranch, but Seth had chosen to build a new home on the other side of the property. Nina, the youngest of the Montgomery siblings, was away at nursing school, the last Cassie had heard.

She let out a weary sigh. So many memories. So much of her childhood had been spent here. It had essentially been her second home. She missed this place. Missed this family whom she'd loved as if it had been her own. Her heart stuttered. How she missed Ella. She couldn't help but wonder how different things would be if Ella hadn't gotten sick.

Surely they would still be the best of friends. Maybe even sisters-in-law by now. She shook her head, discarding the fanciful thoughts. Even if Ella hadn't gotten sick, there was no telling if Cassie and Eric could've made a relationship work.

Besides, if they had stayed together, he never would've met Lorelei. And while that would mean he wouldn't be in the predicament he was in now, it would also mean he wouldn't have Wyatt. Cassie had no doubt his son already meant the world to him.

Somehow, God had a way of making everything work out how it was supposed to. Even if it didn't make sense at the time.

She had called Eric to warn him she was coming, and she hadn't given him a chance to decline. Now, less than twenty minutes later, she was here, ringing his doorbell. In the few moments she stood waiting, she couldn't help but notice the lovely view hadn't changed. Two Adirondack chairs overlooked a seemingly endless pasture filled with splotches of bright wildflowers.

Despite the calming scene, her heart raced. She had been stopped by a patrol car at the end of the driveway. Eric had the foresight to warn the officer she was coming, so she'd been allowed to pass. Still, she worried someone was watching. She felt incredibly vulnerable. What if the men from last night had come onto Eric's property on foot? The ranch was thousands of acres. It was impossible to patrol it all. So many points of entry. So many places for an attacker to lie low. What if they were hiding behind the barn? Or camouflaged amid the junipers? What if she was in their sights right now? What if—

She jumped when Eric swung the door open. He wore a cozy-looking navy blue flannel shirt, untucked, and a pair of faded jeans. His nearly black hair was mussed and shadows rested below his coffee-colored eyes, indicating he hadn't slept well. She certainly couldn't blame him. The sight of him, weary and worn, tugged at her heart.

She felt empathy, she assured herself. Nothing more.

"Come on in," he said, his voice low. "Wyatt didn't sleep much last night. I don't know if it's because he napped late or if it's because his life has been thrown into complete chaos. Regardless, he's sleeping now, so we have some time to talk."

She gratefully stepped into the safety of his home, relishing the aroma of coffee that clung to the air. She'd gulped down a quick cup before heading over here this morning, but the way exhaustion was nagging at her, she could certainly use a bit more caffeine.

"How are you doing?" Genuine concern seeped into his expression. "How's your head?"

"It's fine." There was still a dull ache, but it was nothing compared to what Eric was going through. The bump on her head was the least of her concerns right now. "How are *you*?"

"Ready for another cup of coffee." He dodged what he knew she was asking. "Would you care for some?"

He didn't want to talk about the fact that Lorelei was dead. Not just dead, but murdered. Strangled. At least, that was the initial assessment due to the ligature marks on her neck. She shuddered.

Their small town had its share of crime these days, as so many places across the country seemed to. Yet, thankfully, murders were rare. No doubt the news of a body pulled out of the river would leave people reeling.

"Yes, I'd love a cup of coffee." She let her question about his welfare drop and followed him into the kitchen, pulled out a chair at the table and dropped down into it. Cassie clutched the folder as Eric poured two mugs of coffee.

He set one in front of her, then dropped into the seat across from her, eyeing the folder with curiosity.

She placed the information on the table and took a sip of the hot brew, grateful for the extra few moments it bought her.

"What did you find?" Eric demanded, his eyes on the folder. "You said it was important."

She set her mug down. It was best to get this over with, best to get everything out in the open.

"It's easier if I show you," Cassie said, her tone apologetic. Eric had already been through so much the past few days. She was about to pummel him with more bad news, but it couldn't be helped. He deserved to know.

She pulled out a copy of a newspaper article. She watched as his eyes scanned the headline, Rollover Crash Kills One. Before he could question the importance of that, or read the article in its entirety, she pulled out another sheet. An obituary posted on a funeral home website. In the upper right-hand corner was a picture of a pretty young brunette.

"You found another Lorelei Coffman?" he asked in confusion.

"Not exactly. This Lorelei Rose Coffman is from Goodrich, Wisconsin. She was born on April sixteenth, and she'd be twenty-six. Just like your notes stated."

He stared at her, clearly not comprehending where she was going with this.

"Are you sure Lorelei was from Goodrich?"

"That's what she told me."

"Did you ever see her driver's license?" she pressed. "Did you ever see her picture?"

He shrugged. "I don't think so. I never had reason to. In all the years I've known *you*, I've never seen *your* driver's license. It's not something people walk around sharing. What are you getting at?"

"There's no easy way to say this, Eric, but I don't believe Lorelei was Lorelei at all. I spent hours looking into this last night." She paused, feeling pained, but pushed ahead. "This woman was killed in an accident less than a year before you met your Lorelei…or whoever she was. My best guess? I think Wyatt's mother stole this woman's identity. Or, more likely, she bought this woman's identity off the dark web."

Eric dropped his gaze, staring at the pages for a moment. Cassie's words seemed to bounce through his mind, but at first, he was unable to grasp them. He allowed them to play over and over on a constant loop

I think Wyatt's mother stole this woman's identity.

She wouldn't have. She *couldn't* have. Right? That was too much. Too far-fetched.

"Eric," she said softly, reaching over to squeeze his hand, "did you hear me?"

"I heard you," he muttered angrily, finally lifting his gaze. She flinched, drawing her hand back. "I'm struggling to make sense of what you said." He wasn't sure if he was angry at Cassie, angry at Lorelei—or whoever she was—or simply angry at the situation. "I don't believe you. That can't be right."

Only, maybe she was right. He seemed to be staring at the proof of her suspicion. In his heart he knew

Cassie wouldn't make this type of accusation unless she was sure.

"I searched the DMF database," she said, all business. "I know what I'm talking about."

"DMF?" he echoed.

"Death Master File. It's a database run by the Social Security Administration. The information you gave me matches *this* Lorelei." She tapped the obituary again, trying to emphasize what he wasn't able to comprehend. "Both women are similar in height, build and coloring. It wouldn't be difficult for your Lorelei to pass as this one. I have a hunch she purchased this woman's driver's license. There's a market for that kind of thing, if you have the right connections. They look similar enough she could have gotten away with it if no one scrutinized it. I ran several other searches in different databases, but I keep coming back to the same conclusion."

"You believe Lorelei isn't really Lorelei," he said, his tone dull. And while part of his brain was screaming that couldn't be true, a little whisper floating through his mind told him that it very well could be. "Then who was she?"

He dragged a hand through his hair. Who was this woman? Someone who had the type of connections to buy a fake identity? And now she was gone. Dead. Visions of her lifeless body flitted through his mind, but he shoved them away.

Cassie pulled her laptop toward her. "I knew this would be hard to grasp. That's why I brought my computer. I can show you everything I looked through so you can see it for yourself."

He shook his head, already feeling overwhelmed. Resignedly he said, "That's okay. The file is enough."

"I don't know who she was," Cassie admitted, her tone softening now that her point was made. "This is as far as I got with my search. I thought you should know right away what I found. I can tell you that Lorelei—your Lorelei, to clarify—seemed to have disappeared completely the day she left Mulberry Creek four years ago. I've checked her financials. There's nothing. No credit card use. No bank statements. No tax return filed with the IRS. I can't even find so much as a cell phone connected to her name. It's as if she disappeared into thin air when she left town."

"How is that possible?"

Cassie winced. "Given what I uncovered last night, I think it's likely she took on a new identity. Everything I've found suggests she did it once. It only makes sense that because she disappeared so completely, she did it again. The only thing I could trace to her was Wyatt's birth certificate. But even that stood alone. I couldn't find a rental agreement, a vehicle title. Nothing. It's as if she wanted Lorelei Coffman on that document but nothing else. I think, in her own way, she wanted you to have that tie to Wyatt."

"I can't believe this. Now she's dead. Am I ever going to get answers?"

"I'll do whatever I can to help you." Cassie paused a moment. Then, in a soft, worried voice, she asked, "Eric, are you a suspect?"

He felt as if his mind was moving in slow motion, because, again, it took him a moment to comprehend what she was saying. A suspect. In the death of a woman he'd dated. A suspect in the death of Wyatt's mother. The thought sickened him, but he understood why she was asking.

He shook his head. "I don't think so. Nothing the detective said to me yesterday after we left the morgue led me to think so. They estimate her time of death to be shortly after she left Wyatt with me. Right around that time, I was trying to file a police report, but she hadn't been gone long enough." He paused. "Being shot at yesterday only confirms that there are some dangerous characters in town." His brow furrowed. "I haven't seen her in years. It's been ages since I even thought about her. But I certainly didn't want her dead."

"Of course you didn't."

Eric's phone, which was resting next to the coffeepot, rang. He wearily got to his feet to answer it. He glanced at the screen. "It's Detective Bianchi."

"Hopefully he has information."

"This is Eric," he said, by way of greeting.

"Hey, Eric, Detective Bianchi here. Would it be okay if I stopped by in a bit? I told you I'd contact you if I had any news." He hesitated. "I think we've uncovered something about, uh, Lorelei. Something I'd feel better telling you in person."

"Would this information happen to be in regard to the fact that Lorelei isn't really Lorelei at all?" Eric guessed as his gaze locked with Cassie's.

"You knew?" the detective asked, his tone gruff.

"Not until a few minutes ago," Eric admitted. "The file I shared with you, well, I shared it with Cassie, too. She's here right now."

"Ahhh," the detective said. "You know that there's a Lorelei Coffman, deceased, out of Wisconsin that matches her description."

"I know that now."

"Did Ms. Anderson have anything else to share?"

"That was it, so far."

"I assume that's got to be shocking," Detective Bianchi replied.

"To say the least," Eric muttered.

"I was going to look into her claim that she'd been in foster care," the detective continued, "but given this newest information, that seems pointless."

"Agreed." Why look into an identity that was fake?

"Let me know if anything else comes up, and I'll do the same." Detective Bianchi disconnected.

Before Eric could take his seat again, the doorbell rang. It was still early, and yet he felt as if he had a full day in. He was already exhausted, and no amount of coffee was going to help with that.

"Expecting someone?" Cassie asked.

"My parents. They were on vacation, spending a few weeks with some retired friends in Colorado, but I called them yesterday and asked them to come home. After we were shot at, I maybe should've told them to stay away, but I didn't want to tell them about Lorelei or Wyatt over the phone. I also didn't want them to hear it from someone else, if news got out before they got back."

Cassie moved to rise, but he motioned her back to her seat.

"Drink your coffee," he insisted, needing a few moments alone with his parents to break the news to them. "We'll join you shortly."

He trudged toward the door, feeling as if he'd been drowning in a nightmare he couldn't awake from. When he pulled it open, he found a small comfort in seeing his parents' familiar faces.

"What's happened?" Julia Montgomery demanded as she sidestepped him and moved into the entryway.

"Your cryptic request that your father and I cut our vacation short and come home scared the daylights out of me."

"A little more information would've been appreciated," his dad, James, agreed.

"I know," Eric said. "This just isn't a conversation I wanted to have on the phone."

Julia placed her hands on her hips, scanned him up and down, as if to determine he was safe from harm.

Before Eric could say anything by way of explanation, Wyatt, still dressed in dinosaur pajamas, appeared at the top of the stairs. He was hugging a tattered bear that had been in the suitcase he arrived with.

"Daddy, I'm hungry," he announced, rubbing his eyes and seemingly unaware of their visitors. He began to carefully plod down the staircase.

"Daddy?" Julia echoed, her eyes wide as she took in the sight of her grandson for the first time. She let out a small huff of disbelief, then turned to Eric, silently begging for answers.

"We have a grandson?" James demanded, his voice low and full of awe.

"I'll get him breakfast," Cassie said as she appeared in the kitchen doorway. She gave a hesitant wave to his parents, then headed over to Wyatt.

"Cassie?" Julia's confused gaze darted between Eric, Cassie and Wyatt.

He needed to clarify the situation immediately before his parents' heads took off with crazy ideas. Already it looked as if they were trying to connect dots that didn't exist.

"Yes, Cassie, if you could make some toast for Wyatt, I'd appreciate it. He likes peanut butter. No jelly." He had discovered that yesterday, the hard way, when his son had something akin to a tantrum over the matter. He watched as Cassie guided Wyatt into the kitchen.

Julia clutched James's arm. "We have a grandson named Wyatt." Her voice trembled.

"Wyatt?" James echoed. "Named after your granddad?"

"Yes." Lorelei had told him that. It was one of the few things she'd had time to admit to before her hasty escape. She had named their son after his father's father, whom she'd known Eric had been close to before he died. Maybe the woman hadn't been completely heartless.

Julia turned to Eric. "I didn't think you and Cassie were speaking. What's going on here?"

"Lorelei stopped by a few nights ago," he began. "Do you remember Lorelei?"

"I do," his mother said carefully, her eyes narrowing. "The girl you thought you were crazy about, but then she up and left, no goodbye? No forwarding address?"

"That would be the one."

Relieved that Cassie was keeping Wyatt occupied, he gently explained the whole, awful tale to his parents. Starting with Wyatt's arrival, the only good thing to come out of the last few days, and ending with Cassie's discovery that Lorelei had stolen someone's identity.

"I can't believe she's dead. *Murdered*," Julia moaned.

"I can't believe she kept your son from you," James added. "How could she do something so despicable? Where has she been all these years?"

"I'd like answers to those questions as well." Eric's phone, which he still clutched in his hand, rang again. This time, it was his doctor's office calling. He excused himself to answer it. Heart pounding, knees feeling a bit too weak, he listened as the receptionist explained his doctor had put a rush on the paternity test. The results had just arrived. He needed to come to the office because it was their policy not to give results over the phone. His other option was to wait and they would send the results in the mail.

He was *not* going to wait.

Five minutes later, it was decided that his parents would stay with Wyatt. Despite the circumstances, they were overjoyed to have a grandson and anxious to spend time with him. Cassie had volunteered to accompany him to the doctor's office to provide moral support. He didn't think he needed the support, as he was sure he knew what the results would be, but he appreciated the company.

"I'll check in with the officer at the end of the driveway," Eric said to his parents. "I don't like leaving you here under the circumstances, but I can't wait any longer to confirm Wyatt's mine. I don't doubt it, but I want the proof in my hands."

James eyed the rifle that Eric had perched on the fireplace mantel last night, well out of Wyatt's reach, but close enough to be used should the need arise. He clapped Eric on the back. "Don't worry, son. I'll take care of things here. You go into town, get your answers."

Eric nodded, grateful for his parents' arrival. He may not get all of the answers he craved, but confirming that Wyatt was his son would feel as if one hurdle was out of the way.

"I think your parents are smitten with Wyatt already," Cassie said lightly as they cruised toward town.

"Your dad couldn't take his eyes off him. And your mom couldn't stop smiling."

The rain had started in again. A light sprinkle this time, but enough to require the use of the windshield wipers. Eric gripped the steering wheel of his battered work truck. The thing was a rust bucket that he never took off the ranch. Today, he had no choice. His other truck, the one that had been shot up, had been impounded indefinitely. After that, it would need substantial repairs.

Eric barely heard Cassie's words. He was too distracted by the vehicle that had been behind them for a while. That didn't mean the vehicle was tailing them. It could simply mean they happened to be headed the same direction. It wasn't until just now, when Eric realized how the truck had sped up, closing the distance between them, that he started to worry.

"What's wrong?" Cassie noticed his attention was riveted to the rearview mirror. She twisted around to get a better look. "That truck is flying."

"It is. It's been behind us for several miles. There was a car between us, but it turned off a minute ago. The truck has kept his distance. Until now."

Common sense told Eric something wasn't right about this situation.

"Get down in your seat," he ordered. This couldn't be happening. Fear and anger sizzled through his body. He was putting Cassie's life at risk *again*.

"Why?" Cassie demanded, though she did as he requested.

He slouched down as well.

"Because I don't know what's up with that truck." He didn't want to tell her that if they were shot at, slouching down would make them smaller targets. Slouching was hardly a match for a bullet, but why give them clear access to a head shot? An image from yesterday, Cassie's bloody hair, flickered through his mind. He wouldn't be able to live with himself if she was seriously injured, or worse, because of him.

Cassie apparently didn't need further explanation, because she reached for her purse, which was nestled between her feet. Eric instinctively knew she was reaching for her gun. Before she had a chance to pull it out, the big truck nudged Eric's back bumper.

He realized immediately that the little tap was going to cause a big problem. His tires slid across the slick pavement. He hit the brakes, but there was no doubt in his mind that the driver of the vehicle had planned this well. A covered bridge with a concrete guardrail loomed up ahead, growing closer by the second. Eric could see the roiling water of the rain-soaked river raging below.

"Hold on!" he ground out.

Cassie braced her hands against the dashboard.

The truck plowed into them again, this time shoving them toward the steep incline right before the bridge.

Cassie gasped in horror as Eric's truck bumped and jostled.

Eric was only vaguely aware of the other truck roaring by as it passed them. It felt as if his world was moving in fast-forward as his own truck spun out of control.

Quicker than he could blink, his old vehicle was careening down the hill, racing toward the swollen, churning water.

FOUR

They hit the roaring water with a bone-jarring jolt. Cassie gripped the dashboard, trying to hold steady as the clunky old truck bobbed roughly on the surface of the choppy river. Icy water streamed in through the gaps in the floorboards, gushing over her feet, instantly making them tingle. She sucked in a surprised breath, shock swirling through her as her mind tried to process what had happened. She was only vaguely aware that the engine sputtered, then died.

"Roll down your window," Eric demanded.

She swiveled her attention to her door, where she found an old-style window crank, the likes of which hadn't been installed in vehicles for, well, she didn't know how long. A few decades? She made quick work of the task, as did Eric.

"I don't think the river is all that deep," she noted, finally gathering her wits about her. "If it was deep, we'd be submerged. I think we're hitting the bottom and bouncing along."

"I think so, too. It's usually pretty shallow, but with the recent rain, this is the fullest I've seen it lately. The problem is that it's flowing so fast."

"Right," Cassie agreed. If they tried to get out, they'd

be washed away. Or potentially washed under the truck, where they'd surely meet their end. She corkscrewed her neck, trying to get a view of the road.

The truck was parked off to the side. The window was rolled down. Cassie couldn't make out the driver or the passenger, but she could make out the barrel of a rifle sticking out of the window frame.

"Down!" she shouted as she nearly folded herself in half.

Eric followed suit.

Boom!

The truck jolted, listed precariously to the side in that moment, and the gunshot went wide.

She may have whimpered—she was too rattled to pray, but she knew God would hear her heart's desperate cry.

Another shot rang out, and the metallic clang suggested it blasted the tailgate. The man shooting was above them, at an awkward angle, and Cassie assumed the bullet went through the truck and, thankfully, hit the riverbed.

She dared to lift her head enough to peek out the open passenger window, Ruger at the ready. She hated the idea of shooting someone, but she would defend herself and Eric.

"We've rounded a bend in the river." Relief coursed through her. No wonder the man had missed. He'd lost his chance at a clear shot. She sat up cautiously, looking out the back window now. "I don't see them anymore."

The truck bobbed viciously, and she knew the gunman wasn't the only threat.

Even though she didn't think they were in danger of the truck becoming completely submerged, she wasn't naive enough to think they were safe yet. They weren't. Not even close.

"I think we'll be okay," Eric said, his tone careful. "As long as this old thing doesn't roll. If it rolls…"

He didn't have to finish that sentence. If it rolled, it would drag them under, and given the ferocity of the current, they'd have a terrible time trying to pull themselves out.

The truck continued to bounce along around another bend, and Cassie spotted the fallen tree, hanging partially over the water, a moment before the truck slammed into it. The impact was so intense she flew forward, then back, her seat belt the only thing saving her from being flung into the windshield.

The water crept higher, sloshing around their waists with every jolt of the truck. It was so cold, but Cassie knew that was the least of their concerns at the moment.

She pulled her phone out of her purse.

"There's no time. We need to move," Eric ground out. "Now. That tree is holding us in place, but it's only a matter of time before it gives way."

And only a matter of time before the pursuers would make another appearance. Neither of them had to say it, but they were both thinking it.

They scrambled to unbuckle their seat belts, and then Eric gave Cassie a nudge.

"We'll go out your window. You're closest to the embankment."

Cassie nodded, not wasting time, and maneuvered herself so she was standing, crouched on the seat. She looped her purse strap around her neck, not willing to leave her weapon behind.

She put one foot on the window frame and leaned out. The riverbank was too far for her to reach. If she jumped, she wouldn't make it. The truck bobbed precariously, and she knew she was wasting precious seconds as she tried to decide what to do.

The truck listed to the side, responding to her weight. The movement caused the vehicle to jolt forward, and Cassie braced herself, fearful it would slam into the fallen tree, break it and hurl them forward. Instead, the movement jerked them sideways.

"Cassie, hurry," Eric urged.

She glanced over her shoulder. He was pressed against his door, trying to counteract her weight with his own, attempting to balance out the truck.

"I'm going." She gripped the opening of the window with both hands and hoisted herself as gently as she could through the opening. "That movement twisted us enough that I can use the tree as a bridge."

The water swirled menacingly beneath her. If she fell in, she would surely be dragged under. Branches scratched across her face, but as she so very carefully reached out with one soaked jean-clad leg, while balancing with one foot on the window frame, her other foot made contact with the old tree. Holding on to the sturdiest branch she could reach, she pulled herself out of the truck. With her drenched clothing pasted to her body, weighing her down, it wasn't an easy task.

She was all too aware that Eric was still inside, and any sudden movement on her part could send the truck careening off-kilter again. Yet they had to hurry. She knew they hadn't seen the last of the men who'd run them off the road.

With another desperate plea to God, she found both

feet firmly planted on the tree. The old thing groaned, undoubtedly from her weight as well as the pressure of the vehicle. She moved along it, toward the shore, checking for Eric.

"I'm right behind you," he assured her as he appeared in the wobbling truck's open window frame.

She moved along the tree gingerly, weaving around branches, watching her footing, acutely aware that Eric hadn't left the truck yet. Without stopping, she shot him a questioning look.

"I'm afraid the tree won't hold us both," he said. "But at least now the truck is lodged against it, so I don't think it'll roll."

Unless the tree breaks.

In moments that felt like an eternity, she reached the riverbank. Whipping her head around, she watched in horror as the tree dipped under Eric's weight. The truck made a grating sound, then the tree creaked, and she instinctively knew something terrible was about to happen.

With both feet on the bobbing tree, Eric rushed forward, struggling to make his way through the maze of branches. A horrendous sound filled the air as the tree split, finally unable to withstand the truck's weight. The vehicle surged forward, pulling the broken tree with it.

Cassie reached out as Eric leaped toward her. Her pulse hammered. They were so close to escaping this ordeal. Her heart would break if she lost him now. She shoved away horrible visions of Eric tumbling into the river and willed him to make it to her.

"Come on!" she cried.

The tree jerked, a branch shooting sideways, catching Eric in the arm. He grunted in pain. The impact almost knocked him back into the water, but his hand latched on to Cassie's, and she jerked him onto dry land.

"Thank You, Lord," she whispered, meaning it with every ounce of her being. Despite the years of silence between them, losing him would've been devastating.

The truck flipped then, rolling, filling with water. The remainder of the tree twisted, struggling against the current.

"We can't stay here," Cassie said.

Eric was breathing hard. He had been only moments away from being pulled under. Cassie couldn't bear to think about that.

"Let's move." His gaze darted around, scouring the forest.

"One step ahead of you," Cassie said lightly as she took off.

"I know where we are. We didn't get too far downstream. Bud Jones's place should be this way. He's a wheat farmer, and his field is right on the other side of these trees. Though I don't like the idea of being out in the open."

Cassie agreed. This early in the year, the field would still be mostly bare. She couldn't stop looking over her shoulder as they hustled through the woods. She noted Eric doing the same, so she knew she wasn't alone in her fear that they were still being pursued.

They had only been rushing through the foliage for a few minutes when Cassie glanced down and let out a gasp of horror.

"Eric, what happened?" she demanded. She realized then that he was holding his left arm with his right hand. Blood dribbled through his fingers. It hit the ground, adding to the blood trail she now realized they were leaving behind.

"The tree," he said, by way of explanation. "When it hit me, it gouged my arm."

"I don't have a good feeling about this." Though they hadn't seen their attackers, she couldn't shake the suspicion that they were being stalked. Especially now that she realized Eric's wound could lead the criminals right to them. Because surely, by now, if they were being followed, the men would have spotted the partially submerged truck. And from there, the blood.

"Let's keep going." Eric plowed ahead. "I have an idea."

"But your arm—"

"Don't worry about it." He glanced over his shoulder and frowned at the bright red droplets shimmering against the shrubbery leaves. "We'll make it work to our advantage."

He took off, and Cassie hustled after him. Finally they came out of the woods. She frowned at what looked to be a junkyard.

"I thought you said this belonged to a farmer." She scanned the area. The weed-infested field was full of the carcasses of old tractors and other miscellaneous rusted-out farm equipment.

"It does. We haven't reached his actual farmland, but old Bud is known for not being able to part with things. I guess you could say he's part farmer, part hoarder."

Eric jogged out of the tree line and into the metal graveyard. He beelined his way to an old truck, baby blue but rusted almost beyond recognition. As soon as he neared it, he slapped his bloody hand against the largest robin's-egg blue patch of paint left on the door.

"What are you doing?" Cassie demanded. She did not like being out in the open like this and was tempted to dart behind a decrepit tractor.

Without answering, Eric whipped off his flannel shirt, leaving only his white T-shirt behind. Cassie was startled at the amount of blood the fabric had absorbed. He quickly wrapped the flannel shirt around the gash, finally cutting off the droplets of blood that had been spattering.

"Follow me," Eric ordered.

Cassie didn't argue because it seemed as if he had a plan. They *needed* a plan. She trotted after him as he went back to the tree line. Instead of darting back to the vicinity from which they'd emerged, he jogged another thirty feet or so, then cut back into the trees.

Cassie could see a farmhouse in the distance and had expected them to continue moving toward it. Instead, Eric grabbed her hand and tugged her toward a rusted-out loader bucket that was just inside the trees along with some other smaller, equally ancient farm equipment. They slid behind it, crouching.

Waiting.

Watching.

They didn't have a very clear view as the leaves and pine boughs blocked their line of sight. But they didn't need a clear view to make out the shape of two men who crept from the forest right where Cassie and Eric had emerged not that long ago. The men pointed to the ground, likely at the trail Eric had inadvertently left behind.

Cassie darted a glance at Eric. He glared at the men,

likely wishing he had a way to take them down. She carefully unzipped her purse and pulled out her weapon. Eric's head whipped her way.

Protection, she mouthed.

He nodded.

She wouldn't shoot the men. Not unless she had to. But she certainly wouldn't sit here defenseless.

It was easy to tell the moment the two men spotted the bloody handprint on the rusted vehicle. One man gave the other a shove, then pressed his finger to his lips, as if indicating silence. Together the two crouched and crept forward, heading straight for the rusted chassis, likely assuming Cassie and Eric were hiding inside.

Just as Eric had intended.

Cassie leaned forward, hoping for a better view. The men weren't wearing hoods, but their features were still obscured by the trees.

Movement beside her grabbed her attention. Eric had his phone out, clearly placing a text. No doubt it was to Detective Bianchi. He scowled, tilting the screen her way. The message did not appear to be going through.

Maybe it would eventually.

Clenching his jaw, Eric held the phone toward the men, this time recording them. The quality would not be good, but Cassie knew he felt he needed to do something.

One man crept around the back of the truck, and the other moved toward the bloodied door, giving it a yank.

The man's cusswords cut through the silence when he realized the truck was empty. The second man—the bald one from the day before, Cassie was sure—lumbered around the vehicle to join his companion. The two men scoured the field, noting all the hiding places among the behemoth piles of rusting equipment.

Then their gaze swung back to the forest. Eric stiffened beside her as they pressed in closer together to find cover behind the bucket.

Cassie prayed the men wouldn't come their way. She didn't want to use her weapon. But if it meant protecting Eric, she would do it. Wyatt had just lost his mother. He could not lose his father, too. And Julia and James had already lost one child. She didn't think they could withstand losing another.

She held her gun at the ready, straining her ears for the sound of footsteps. Of breaking branches or rustling foliage. But she heard nothing.

And then she did.

Grumbling at first.

Muffled conversation.

"They must've run to that farmhouse. This would be so much easier if we could just bring him in dead."

"Well, we can't," the other voice snapped. "The boss wants him alive. You know what he said. The contract is null and void if we kill him. He doesn't care if he's banged up or shot. As long as he can talk."

Cassie's heart gave a jolt, and Eric's face drained of color. Her blood turned to ice in her veins. How could they talk so callously about killing a man? About killing *Eric*? Fear and anger burned fast and bright through her.

"You better be more careful," the second voice continued. "You know he said if we hurt the kid he'll skin us alive."

"I know," the bald man grumbled. "That's why I didn't take the shot yesterday. But pushing them into the river was a bonehead move. They could've drowned. If I lose out on my payday because of you, you're going to be sorry."

"Yeah? What're you gonna do about it?" the other man taunted.

She caught a glimpse of him then. Thin, shaggy hair. Not much to go on.

"You gonna try to take me out, too?" he continued.

"I might. I could handle this job on my own just fine."

Snide laughter was followed by, "You think so? You're nothing but a loser. You would never get the job done without me."

The men continued trudging through the forest, and Cassie couldn't make out any more of their squabbling.

For a moment she wanted to chase after them. Let the hunters become the hunted. She longed to find out who they were, where they had come from and what the "boss" wanted with Eric. But to do so would be foolish. It wasn't in her repertoire to take down two dangerous men.

Having outwitted them would have to be enough. For now.

"I can't believe I just let them get away," Eric growled to himself.

The men were out of sight now.

Cassie and Eric had stayed put for a good five minutes, which felt more like five hours, to be sure the men weren't lurking in the woods.

When they finally decided it was as safe as it was going to get, they rose from their hiding spot.

"We had no choice," Cassie said firmly. "I certainly wasn't about to chase two armed men through the woods. Especially when they have no qualms about shooting you."

Eric knew she was right.

But that didn't mean he had to like it.

"At least I know they don't want me dead," he said dryly. Yet remembering their conversation made his heart pound. Who could these people possibly be? Who was their boss? What could he want to talk to Eric about? Certainly nothing good. He could barely wrap his mind around the fact that someone was after him. It wasn't as if he had answers to anything. All he had were questions.

His phone vibrated in his hand. He glanced at it as they made their way through the woods, closer to the farm.

"My text finally went through," he told Cassie. "Detective Bianchi is on the way to get us. He's sending some men out to look for that old battered truck that hit us. I didn't have much to go on, just that it was an older-model green Ford."

"It'll have a dented bumper."

"Right. But by the time my text went through, I'm guessing they got a head start." He paused the conversation but kept walking as he tapped against his phone screen again. "I'm telling the detective to meet us down the road. No reason to drag Bud Jones into this. Don't want to get the man riled up, and I sure don't want to cause any trouble for him. Best if he doesn't know what went down on his property."

Eric also knew Bud was a horrible gossip, and the last thing Eric needed right now was half the town speculating on the confusion that had become his life.

Fifteen minutes later, an unmarked navy sedan

pulled over to the side of the road, just down from Bud's driveway.

"We need to get you to your doctor," Cassie said as they rushed to the car. "And not just for the paternity test results."

He glanced at her over the roof before tugging the door open. "I think you're right. I'm pretty sure I'm going to need stitches."

His arm throbbed something fierce, but he knew the outcome could've been so much worse. He was grateful he'd gotten away with nothing but a sizable gash.

Once they were settled inside, Detective Bianchi twisted around to face them.

"The video you took finally came through. I can't make much of it out," he said.

"I knew it was a long shot," Eric admitted.

"I've got someone working on it, trying to see if there's any point when the leaves aren't in the way. Maybe they can get a clear shot of their faces, enhance it some. Same guys as yesterday?"

"I think so." Eric glanced at Cassie for confirmation.

"One of the men today was bald, so I'd say so. Though I never got a look at all at the other guy yesterday. He was taller, thinner than the bald one," she said.

"Sandy hair, kind of shaggy," Eric added. "But I didn't get a clear look at his face, either."

"I've had my men looking for the vehicle you described, but they haven't spotted it yet. They went straight to the covered bridge, but they were long gone."

"Of course they were," Eric muttered.

"We did overhear a conversation, though." Cassie relayed what they had heard to the detective.

He nodded. "It doesn't surprise me that someone hired them. Interesting that they want you alive."

Interesting is one way to look at it.

"The boss man must think you know something." The detective looked over his shoulder and leveled his gaze on Eric for a moment. "Are you sure you have no idea what this is about?"

As much as the words needled him, Eric couldn't blame the detective for asking. It was his job to look at the situation from all angles.

"I wish I did," Eric said honestly. "I have to assume this has to do with Lorelei. But if they think I have answers about anything, they couldn't be more wrong."

"I have other news," the detective said grimly.

"About Lorelei?" Eric demanded.

The detective slid his gaze to Cassie. "I was just made aware of a call this morning from a Mr. Kirkwood."

Cassie leaned forward. "My neighbor Mr. Kirkwood?"

"Yes," Detective Bianchi said. "He called in to report a suspicious man prowling around your house. Apparently Mr. Kirkwood can see your back deck from one of his upstairs windows. A man, wearing a hood pulled low, was trying to open your back door. Mr. Kirkwood opened the window and shouted at him, asking what he was doing. The man took off, jumped your fence and disappeared. Your neighbor called 911, but by the time we got someone over there, there was no sign of him. Another one of your neighbors remembers a dark SUV being parked on the curb and a guy getting into it. But she said she wasn't really paying attention. Couldn't recall make or model and didn't really have a description of the guy, other than that he wore a black sweatshirt. This all happened well before the incident in the river, so I suspect one of the men was pulling double duty today."

"That confirms Cassie is on their radar now," Eric said, his tone grim. It was one thing when they'd been targeting Cassie because she was with him. But this proved beyond a doubt that they knew who she was and that they were going to go after her as well.

His gut clenched as an unwanted vision of Lorelei, lifeless, lying on the morgue table, flashed into his mind. In that moment he wanted to reach out and pull Cassie into his arms, assure himself that she was fine. Very much alive and that these men wouldn't get her.

He restrained himself and focused on calming his frantic heart instead.

"It does," Detective Bianchi said. "In unrelated news, we've got two missing girls. It appears they're runaways, but we've had some trouble with human trafficking in this area."

"Here?" Eric asked in disbelief. "In Mulberry Creek?"

"It's become a problem everywhere," Cassie said from beside him.

"It has," the detective agreed. "The problem is, our department—a lot of departments—are just stretched too thin these days. I wish I had more people to put on your case."

"But you also need to focus on the missing girls," Cassie said

"Do you think the two cases are related?"

"Not at all, Eric," the detective said firmly. "I'm only bringing it up because I want you to know that while I wish I could concentrate solely on your case, I can't."

The man, who couldn't have been much older than Eric, looked weary beyond his years.

"Don't get me wrong," the detective said. "The department is looking into Lorelei's death. We're investigating these attacks on the two of you, trying to find these men."

"But you have your hands pretty full right now," Eric surmised.

"Yeah," Detective Bianchi ground out. "We sure do. Our department is small, and I'm the only detective on staff. I wish we could put a few more people out at the ranch. But crime is up, and there's a shortage of officers just about everywhere."

"I get it," Eric said. "You just don't have the manpower."

"We're doing our best. We pulled fingerprints off the Jane Doe—"

"Lorelei," Eric automatically corrected. "I mean, I know technically she's a Jane Doe at this point. But she's Wyatt's mother. She deserves a name of her own." He knew that whoever this woman turned out to be, if they ever found out, she would always be Lorelei Coffman to him.

The detective cleared his throat and continued. "We pulled prints from Lorelei, ran them through IAFIS."

"A national fingerprint database," Cassie told Eric under her breath.

"But we didn't get a match," the detective continued.

"At least she's not a criminal," Eric said. Then thought better of it. Identity theft was, in itself, a crime. "I take that back. She'd never been caught, at least."

"People get fingerprinted for other things," Cassie offered up. "Prospective foster and adoptive parents have to be fingerprinted as part of a background check. More and more employers are requiring it as well."

"Regardless," Detective Bianchi said as they turned onto the road that would lead to the clinic, "she's not in the system. We've hit another dead end."

Eric glanced at Cassie. Determination flashed in her eyes, and he was grateful. Despite the risk, he was relieved that he had C. J. Anderson, private investigator, on his side and ready to help him solve this case. Because, at the rate things were going, and with the department bogged down with other cases, he needed all the help he could get.

FIVE

"Are you all right?" Cassie asked Eric as they stepped out of the clinic. She glanced around, looking for anything suspicious.

A cruiser waited in the parking lot. Detective Bianchi had dropped them off—had questioned them quite thoroughly in the parking lot before letting them go inside—but had requested that Officer Hughes drive them home, since Eric was down another vehicle.

She stopped at the end of the sidewalk, wanting a moment alone with Eric.

"I'm fine." He gingerly rubbed his arm. "The shot they gave me to numb it up really helped."

She gently fluttered her fingers over his hand, the one covering the wound now held together with stitches. Then she crossed her arms over her stomach, reminding herself that the more distance, both physical and emotional, she kept from Eric, the better. Seeing him again brought up too many old memories, so many emotions. It would be easy to fall for him again, but that could not happen. She knew better than to risk her heart on a man who pushed her away. Yet that mental reminder couldn't stop her from checking in on him.

"I'm not talking about your arm and you know it," she said quietly.

He blew out a beleaguered sigh and didn't look at her.

"Yeah. I'm fine," he repeated. "I mean, why wouldn't I be? I just found out I have a three-year-old son. The test confirmed it, right? Now I have to come to terms with the fact that I've missed over three years of my child's life. And why? What was the point?"

"I don't know," Cassie softly admitted. She wasn't going to suggest Lorelei had a good reason. Cassie couldn't think of any reason good enough to do what Lorelei had done. "But you have him now. And you're going to be a great dad. You already are."

He continued on as if he hadn't heard her. "I don't understand how she could have kept him from me. Now I'll probably never have answers." Finally his gaze swung to lock on hers. "You have no idea what it feels like to be betrayed like this. Betrayed by someone you loved. Trusted."

Oh, he was so very wrong about that.

"Actually, I do."

"Really?" he scoffed. "Someone kept your child from you, too?"

Cassie gritted her teeth, chafing at his ludicrous remark. She knew he was upset. Lashing out at her because she was the only one there. In an instant, in her mind, they were back in the hospital parking lot. Eric was blaming her for Ella's death. Telling her he'd never forgive her for not doing more.

She slammed a door on those thoughts. She wasn't going to let her mind go there.

"You're right." She pivoted and headed toward the

cruiser. They'd kept Officer Hughes waiting long enough. "You're the only one who has ever been betrayed and lied to."

"Cassie, wait," he said, his tone surprisingly contrite.

His boots slapped against the pavement as he hustled to catch up. She wasn't going to wait. Eric hadn't changed, hadn't grown at all in the years since Ella's death. It would do her well to remember that. She had longed for a future with him once, but she couldn't risk going down that treacherous emotional path again. Yes, she would help him with this case. But she owed him nothing more, not even friendship.

This was a business deal.

That was all.

"I'm sorry," he said as he edged up behind her. "That was rude of me. I'm upset, angry, and I took it out on you. I'm sorry. Really, I am."

She stopped, with her hand on the cruiser's door handle. A bitter breeze picked up, fluttering her hair around her face. She swiped a lock out of her eyes before directing her gaze to Eric.

"I have a habit of doing that," he said sheepishly. "I thought I'd moved past that behavior. But this—" he shook his head "—it's all so much. Too much. Finding out I have Wyatt. Lorelei being—" he winced "—murdered. Now, thanks to me, you're in danger, too," he added contemptuously. "You've been nothing but kind. Helpful. I'm grateful that you're here. Forgive me?"

Maybe he *had* changed. In the past, Eric wouldn't have apologized. He certainly wouldn't have chased after her to do so.

Before she could reply, Officer Hughes buzzed her window down. "Everything okay?"

"It's fine." Cassie tugged the door open. Not looking at Eric, she said, "We shouldn't keep the officer waiting any longer."

She slid into the car's back seat, while Eric took the front.

"We found the truck," Officer Hughes volunteered. "It was abandoned on a side road not too far from where you went into the river. We were able to trace it back to a mechanic in town. He's got a parking lot full of vehicles he's working on. He didn't even realize it was missing."

"So, it was stolen," Cassie surmised, "which is not helpful at all. Any fingerprints?"

"Too many to be useful," Officer Hughes said. "It looks like several members of the owner's family drove it, along with a mechanic or two at the shop where it was being repaired. But, unfortunately, none of the prints have amounted to anything." She shrugged. "It's possible they wore gloves."

"Another dead end," Eric muttered.

Cassie could feel his frustration.

"They'll mess up sooner or later," Cassie said. "And when they do, they'll be caught."

Eric nodded, but he still looked troubled.

Cassie felt troubled as well. She believed their attackers would be caught. But how much more danger would they face until then?

Eric wasn't surprised by his brother Seth's presence as he and Cassie entered the house. Seth's black Chevy Silverado announced his arrival at the ranch.

What did surprise him was the way Seth grinned

at Cassie, scooped her up and whirled her around theatrically.

Cassie let out a surprised shriek, then laughed.

"It's been a long time, Cassie," Seth said, finally placing her back on her feet. She reached up and ruffled his hair, just like she used to do all those years ago when she and Ella babysat Seth and Nina. Only then, she'd reached down, not up.

Eric was hit by a pang of jealousy.

He wasn't jealous of the way Seth had so casually scooped Cassie into his arms. He was jealous of the ease between the two of them. The carefree delight and camaraderie. He used to have that with Cassie.

Now their past was speckled with ugly memories and tumultuous emotions. He missed their friendship, and while he wasn't naive enough to think a romantic relationship could ever be in their future again, he desperately wanted to move past the awkwardness that seemed to continually creep up on them.

"It's good to see you," Cassie said to Seth as she disentangled herself from his arms. "How did your trip go?"

"Good," he said. "I'm happy with the new bull we got to bring into our program. He comes from prime stock, and he'll be a great addition."

"How are you two?" Julia asked, unable to hold off any longer. Her eyes darted between Cassie and Eric. "I can't believe you were run off the road."

Eric had called his mother on the way home to tell her about their dunk in the river. He didn't want to surprise her with their bedraggled appearance and his bloody shirt. He did not tell her about the men chasing them through the woods or the conversation they'd overheard. She was worried enough, and he thought that information might push her over the edge.

"We made it through okay." Eric kept his tone light.

His mother eyed his shirt. He'd put the flannel back on, the navy color masking the blood in a way his white T-shirt did not.

"Where's Wyatt?" Eric asked, mostly out of genuine concern, but also to take his mother's attention off him.

"Napping," Julia said. "We kept busy while you were gone. We made homemade pizza for lunch. He helped me roll the dough and sprinkle the ingredients. Then we made peanut butter cookies. Your dad played cards with him while I cleaned the kitchen. Our boy can play a mean game of Go Fish."

Eric smiled at that. "Can't wait to play with him."

Julia's gaze darted from her husband to her sons and to Cassie. "I know the circumstances aren't the best. But it warms this mother's heart to have a house full of family again. If only Nina was here."

And Ella, but there was no point in saying it. He hadn't missed how his mom's gaze had landed on Cassie, how her smile had softened when she said the word *family*. Cassie had always been like a third daughter to her.

"How is Nina?" Cassie asked. "I heard she's in nursing school."

"In Bozeman," James said with a nod. "She'll be wrapping it up this spring and then coming home."

"Now catch me up." Seth suddenly became serious. "You two were run off the road on the way to town?"

Eric saw a glimpse of the soldier he'd been.

"Yes, we were."

"I think Mom and Dad told me just about everything, but is there anything you think I should know?" Seth asked Eric.

"You should know I could really use a hand keeping an eye on things around here," Eric said. "And I don't mean the cattle. The detective we've been working with is on a couple of big cases right now. Sounds like the department is spread pretty thin."

He had his back to his mom and gave his brother a look that he hoped Seth would interpret as *I'll catch you up on everything later*. He would tell Seth about the men, about the comment that Eric had to be taken alive but injured wasn't a problem, because it would be good to have his brother on guard.

"You got it." Seth gave Eric a subtle nod. "I'll plan on moving in for the time being. I already took the side-by-side and checked the perimeter. The fence looks good, but I did see questionable tracks along the north line."

"What do you mean?" Eric demanded.

"Large tire tracks, pulled over, half in the ditch where the fence line runs up against Sumac Road. That in itself wasn't too unusual, but due to the rain making the ground soft, I could make out boot prints. Definitely a man's, judging by the size. He walked up to the fence line, then retreated."

Eric frowned. A person could just make out the ranch house from Sumac Road. He could all too easily envision Lorelei's killer checking out the place with a pair of binoculars. Or worse, a rifle scope.

"I hate to say it, but I think until this is over, it's best if we don't leave the house without being armed," Seth suggested.

"I have to agree." Eric glanced at Cassie, then back

at his family. "We also found out there was a guy lurking around Cassie's place, probably trying to break in, but a neighbor scared him off."

"These guys know Cassie is part of this," James surmised. "I'm sure she wasn't hard to track down, but I don't like that at all."

"Nor do I." Julia turned to Cassie. "You need to stay here."

"Oh," Cassie said, her brows furrowing. "I don't know. I'm not sure that's a good idea." Her gaze jumped to Eric.

"You should," he said, relieved his mom had brought it up, because if she hadn't, he would've. "Unless you have somewhere else to go?"

"I don't. But I have a security system. It would've gone off if the man had actually tried to breach my property. I'm also armed. I should be fine. I just—"

"You just need to stay here," James affirmed. "It would be silly not to. There's safety in numbers."

"Besides," Julia said, her tone soothing, "it would ease my mind if you were here, where I know you are safe. If you went home, you know I'd do nothing but worry. Please, for my peace of mind, stay."

Cassie bit her lip, then nodded. Eric knew she was torn but appreciated that she was willing to appease his mother. Julia really would worry.

So would he.

"I'm sure the two of you want to get cleaned up." Julia turned to Cassie. "You'll need something to wear."

Eric's clothes had mostly dried, so he assumed Cassie's had as well. But if hers felt as crunchy with river muck as his did, then she'd definitely want clean clothes.

"I have my suitcase upstairs," his mother continued. "I'm sure I can find something that would fit you. If not, one of the guys can run to our house and raid my wardrobe."

"That's okay," Cassie said. "I keep a duffel bag in my Cherokee. It has a few days' worth of essentials in it. Sometimes while working a case, I find myself needing to stay overnight out of town unexpectedly. I've learned to always be prepared."

"Seth," Julia ordered, "go retrieve Cassie's bag, please. James, would you mind helping me in the kitchen? Wyatt should be up soon. I made an enchilada casserole earlier. I need to slide it in the oven, but we should make a salad."

Julia took off toward the kitchen with James a step behind. Seth went out the front door, after Cassie's bag, before she had a chance to protest.

Suddenly he was alone with Cassie again.

"Thanks for agreeing to stay," he said quietly. "I know it means a lot to my mom."

She frowned.

"And me," he admitted. "I need to know you're safe."

She nodded. "It makes sense for me to stay here. I'm working on the case. It'll be easier to collaborate."

"I don't want it to be awkward between us." Eric wished he'd kept his mouth shut after the clinic visit.

She flashed a forced smile. "There's nothing awkward about it. We're just two old acquaintances, who will temporarily be living under the same roof, trying to stay alive."

"When you put it like that," he began.

She cocked a brow at him. "How else should I put it, Eric? We were never a couple. We never dated. There was never anything between us."

That isn't exactly true. There had been one evening, sheltering in the gazebo during a thunderstorm at a mutual friend's wedding reception, when they'd opened up about their feelings. There had been one shared kiss. A kiss that tilted his world on its axis. A kiss that had left him hoping for more, hoping for a future with Cassie.

She winced, as if knowing exactly where his thoughts had gone. "Maybe if Ella hadn't told us, the very next day, that she was sick… But she did. Everything changed, and there's no going back."

He couldn't argue with that. There was no going back, no matter how badly he wished he could take back the spiteful way he had behaved.

The front door flew open, and Seth sauntered in, holding up a large gray duffel bag. "I assume this is what you need?"

"Yes, thank you." She took the bag from him, then glanced at Eric. "I'll see you at dinner."

She climbed the staircase, disappearing from his sight. Having spent so much time here over the years, she knew her way around as well as he did. She probably even still remembered which cabinet held the pots and pans and which drawer held the silverware.

"I never thought I'd see the two of you in the same room again, let alone the same house," Seth said. "How many years has it been? Five?"

"Six." Not that he'd counted. At least, not on purpose, yet he was acutely aware of the time frame.

"Are you ever going to tell me what happened between the two of you? Growing up, she was here all the time, hanging out with Ella. You got along just fine. Until you didn't."

Eric shook his head. "I acted like an idiot. Said some things I never should have said."

Seth waited, as if assuming he'd continue. When he

didn't, his little brother clapped him on the back. "Cassie is a great person. She was a great friend to Ella, right up to the bitter end. I thought she was a good friend to you, too. See to it that you don't hurt her again."

He strode toward the kitchen, leaving Eric alone with his thoughts and more than a few regrets.

"So, Cassie," Julia began as she swirled her fork through her casserole, "tell me, whatever made you decide to become a private investigator? The last I knew, you were finishing up your business degree. You had an emphasis in finance, if I recall correctly. You were hoping to go into banking."

Eric had wanted an answer to that very question almost from the moment he'd raced into her office. Yet, somehow, he hadn't found a spare minute to ask her. The Cassie he recalled had been a girlie-girl. All pink lip gloss, painted nails and trendy shoes. Her long blond hair had always been styled to perfection.

Now she was still beautiful, but in a more natural way. Her makeup was toned down, her nails bare, her chin-length hair framing her face, bringing out the curves of her cheekbones. Her lean build was more athletic now.

More equipped to run from gunmen, he thought grimly.

He shoved the thought away and zeroed in on what Cassie was saying.

"It's a long story," she replied with a weak smile.

Julia smiled back encouragingly. "We have time. I've missed you. I'd love to get caught up."

Eric glanced at Wyatt. His child and his dad were engaged in a conversation about broccoli at the other end of the table. Wyatt was telling James that broccoli would make them both big and strong.

"It wasn't exactly a planned move," Cassie began. "It came about after Mom died."

Eric vaguely recalled that Maggie Anderson had fallen off her roof while trying to sweep off pine needles. She'd suffered fatal injuries. A wave of guilt washed over him. He'd been so wrapped up in Lorelei and his own grief over Ella at the time, he hadn't even thought to reach out to Cassie. He'd still been too angry.

Too *selfish*, he corrected.

"That was such a horrible accident," Julia murmured. "A surprise to us all."

"It was," Cassie agreed.

Eric felt he should say something, but didn't know what he could say at this point that wouldn't sound trite. So he took a sip of his water and said nothing.

"When I was going through Mom's belongings," Cassie continued, "I found my adoption papers wedged into her Bible."

"I didn't know you were adopted," Eric said, finally finding his voice.

Cassie let out a harsh, quiet laugh. "Neither did I."

"Oh, sweetheart," Julia said, her tone full of compassion. "I'm so sorry. What a way to find out."

Cassie nodded. "It was a shock, all right. My whole life, it was just Mom and me."

Her gaze flicked to his.

His words from earlier in the day came back to slap him upside the head.

You have no idea what it feels like to be betrayed like this. Betrayed by someone you loved. Trusted.

How wrong he had been to say such a thing. Cassie

did know. She knew all too well. He remembered how close she and her mom had been.

"That had to have been tough," he said quietly.

"It was. To cut the story down just a bit, I decided to find my birth mother. Only it wasn't so easy. It took months of research, of going down dead-end roads and chasing false leads. But, eventually, I found her. Her name's Danae Schroeder, and she lives in a small town in South Dakota. I have two half brothers. One is a senior in high school, and the other a college sophomore."

Her lips quirked up in a smile then, and Eric felt a sense of relief. Perhaps despite the rocky start, this story had a nice ending.

"Have you met them?" James asked. Though he'd been chatting with Wyatt, he'd clearly been paying attention to Cassie's tale.

"I have. I wouldn't say we're close, but we're cordial. I was a shock to them at first, but they seem to have adjusted to the fact that they have a big sister."

Eric had so many questions. Had her birth mother been happy to see her? Why had she been given up? How was Cassie handling the fact that Maggie had kept something so monumental from her? But he didn't have the right to ask any of those things.

"Goodness," Julia said. "I don't even know what to say. I didn't realize I was asking such a personal question. I thought perhaps your interest in private investigating had been sparked by a news report or something of that nature. I didn't mean to pry. But I am glad that you shared this with us."

"It's been an interesting journey," Cassie admitted. "When I started looking, I joined message boards with other adoptees looking for their birth parents. Once I found Danae, I started helping others. I found out I was good at it. I decided to use some of my inheritance from my mom to open my own business."

"Your PI business," Julia said approvingly.

"I already had my business degree by that point, so the next step was to become licensed as a private investigator, and now, a few years later, here I am."

"Good for you." James grinned. "I always knew you had a lot of spunk."

"I'm sure learning you were adopted was devastating at first," Julia said, "but that's just like God to turn all things for good. You took your own pain and used it to create a business that helps people."

"Yes, I suppose I did. My specialty is helping adoptees find their birth parents. And vice versa—I've helped a few birth parents find the children they gave up. But I've also done my fair share of tracking down deadbeat dads…and moms. My favorite case to date involved helping a grandmother find her granddaughters, twins, separated at birth."

"It sounds like never a dull moment," James said.

"It isn't." Cassie glanced at Eric, her expression turning grim. "But I've never had a case quite like this."

He thought she probably meant no one had ever tried to kill her before, but they all had too much tact to say that with Wyatt sitting at the table.

"Grammy," Wyatt said, easily using the name Julia had given herself only moments after meeting her grandson, "do we have cookies?"

Julia beamed, probably over the *Grammy* rather than the request for cookies.

"You know we do," she said. "Unless you ate them all when I wasn't looking."

Wyatt's eyes widened, as if shocked by the idea. "I didn't. I saved some for Daddy."

Daddy. There was that word again. He would never tire of it. Not when spoken in that sweet, precious voice.

His mother rose from the table to retrieve the cookies, and everyone else went back to their meal. But Eric couldn't stop thinking that when it came to Cassie, he had quite the habit of putting his foot in his mouth.

Seth was right. Eric needed to be careful, because without meaning to, he seemed to have a knack for hurting Cassie with his words on a daily basis.

They already had a killer after them.

She sure didn't need to have Eric's careless words hurting her, too.

SIX

Eric awoke with a start, his heart pounding and his adrenaline pumping. He glanced at the clock. It was a few minutes before five. Gloomy, dismal predawn light pressed in through the bedroom window. After swinging his legs out of bed, he stood, grabbed the gun he'd left on his nightstand and hustled across his room barefoot. He'd slept in sweats and a T-shirt, just in case something like this happened and he needed to move quickly.

He strained his ears, trying to determine what had awakened him. Times like this, he kind of wished he had a dog.

Why didn't he have a dog?

Now that he had a son, he should have a dog. Every kid needed a dog.

That was a thought to ponder for another time.

For now, he needed to be certain his family was safe. Sure, he had an alarm system. But it was hardly top-notch. Before now, he'd never had the need for anything fancy. Had someone breached it?

He pulled open his door, strained his eyes to see in the semidarkness. The doorways up and down the hallway were all closed.

All but one.

The door to Ella's old room stood open.

The familiar, distant gurgle of his coffeepot settled his racing heart.

With a sigh of relief, he realized Cassie must be up.

He quietly traversed the staircase, not wanting to awaken anyone else in the family. They'd be getting up soon enough. Life on the ranch started early, but he knew everyone was exhausted, both physically and emotionally, from the last few days.

Sure enough, he found Cassie in the kitchen. She, too, looked like she'd just slid out of bed. Her short hair had a wild and crazy look to it that he found oddly appealing. If he was honest with himself, he'd have to admit that he found everything about her appealing.

She wore yoga pants and a sweatshirt. Green-and-purple-striped socks covered her feet. She blew on the steaming mug of coffee she held to her lips and seemed to be lost staring at her laptop screen.

"Working hard already?" Eric asked.

She glanced up at him and smiled, not startled at all, and he wondered if she'd heard him coming.

"I couldn't sleep," she admitted, then took a long sip from her mug.

He nodded and made his way into the kitchen, heading straight for the cupboard that held the coffee cups.

"I hear ya. I had a hard time falling asleep last night." He poured himself a dark, rich cup of the coffee. Cassie clearly knew how to brew the stuff strong, just how he liked it. "What are you working on?"

"I'm just hitting Send," she said, stabbing at the keyboard, "on a report that I've been anxious to get off my plate." She tapped a few more keys, then closed the laptop lid.

He moved to the table and sat across from her. "Find someone's missing parent?"

"Not this time. A woman hired me to trail her husband. She was convinced he was having an affair."

Eric winced. "Do you take those cases often?"

Cassie shrugged. "On occasion. The first case I took didn't turn out well. The man was right. His wife was cheating on him. It left me feeling pretty awful. But he assured me knowing was better than not knowing. I've heard that a lot over the years. That's why I keep taking those cases." Her lips tilted into a small smile. "This case, however, turned out well."

Eric sipped his coffee. "No affair?"

"No affair. Turns out the man had been coming home late, skipping dinners with his wife, to go to the gym. I followed him for a week, like she requested, and that's the only unusual place he ever ended up."

Eric arched a brow in question.

"Long story short, he was feeling like, between his wife's excellent culinary skills—his exact words—and not getting enough exercise, he'd really let himself go. He wanted to surprise her with a trip to the Bahamas for their tenth wedding anniversary. Wanted to be in tip-top shape when they spent their week on the beach."

"He just divulged all that to you?"

"I just happened to end up on the treadmill next to him at the gym. We got talking. Time passes more quickly when you're distracted with chatter."

"Just happened to be on the treadmill next to his?" He gave her a pointed look.

She smirked. "It's all part of the job. Anyhow, I

figured a man who sang his wife's praises to another woman the way he did could not possibly have a philandering heart."

"Especially a beautiful woman," Eric said. Then, realizing he'd said the words out loud, he took another big gulp of his coffee, trying to act as if it was a perfectly normal thing to say. "You let the lady know all was well just now?"

"Yesterday was their anniversary. I didn't want to ruin the guy's surprise, but I didn't want to put off his wife any longer. So yes, I just sent off the report."

"What else are you working on?"

She waved a dismissive hand. "Nothing that can't wait a few more days. Your case is taking top priority."

"Where do we start? Turns out I know so little about Lorelei. How do you investigate someone when you don't even know who they are? *Were*," he amended with a frown, still struggling with the past tense in regard to Lorelei's life.

"It looks as if this case is going to require some good old-fashioned, boots-to-the-ground investigating. I know it may seem invasive, but I need you to tell me everything. Where did you two meet? Did she have any friends in town? How long was she in Mulberry Creek before—"

"Fire!"

The bellowed warning came from Seth. It reverberated through the house, echoing down the staircase.

Eric settled his coffee cup down on the table so fast the scalding liquid sloshed over the side, lightly burning his hands. He barely noticed. He leaped from the chair, and Cassie scrambled to her feet as well.

"It's Mom and Dad's place! Let's move!" Seth shouted as they heard his feet pounding down the staircase.

Eric was already darting across the kitchen, Cassie only a step behind.

Seth and James raced toward the entry as Cassie and Eric joined them.

"Mom and Dad's place is in flames," Seth grated out as he went for his boots. "I was going to go check on the calves and glanced out the window as I was getting ready."

"I'm calling 911," Julia said from the top of the staircase, the phone already pressed to her ear. His mother looked wide-awake despite the fact that she was in her flannel pajamas and her hair was a mess.

The three men shoved their feet into their boots.

Cassie grabbed Eric's arm. "You can't go. What if it's a trap?"

"It probably is," Eric said, "but despite the recent rain, the jack pines around the house could catch fire. It could burn everything on the property, but the closest building is the barn. If the fire reaches the barn, well, the horses are inside because the weather has been so bad."

"I'll come with," Cassie said.

This time, Eric grabbed hold of her arm, stopping her. "No, I need you here. Guard Wyatt?"

He heard the plea, the desperation in his tone. He was no fool. It was doubtful this fire was an accident. Yet it couldn't be ignored. Too much was at stake. What he hadn't said was that the family's photo albums, full of photos of Ella, were in his parents' house. As were all of her keepsakes. Trap or not, those items were precious. Irreplaceable. He needed to do something, but he also had to be sure Wyatt was safe.

Cassie nodded, her eyes locking with his. "With my life," she said vehemently.

On impulse, he leaned forward, pressed a hard, quick kiss to her lips. Their eyes locked briefly, and then Eric grabbed the rifle off the mantel and bolted out the door after his dad and brother.

Cassie stood in the open doorway for just a moment, fingers pressed to her lips as she watched the brothers race to Seth's truck. Eric had kissed her. But she didn't have time to ponder that now. James jogged to the barn, presumably to set the horses free should the worst happen.

A split second later, she shut the door, twisted the dead bolt in place, then raced up the steps to retrieve her Ruger, the surprising kiss all but forgotten in her haste.

Julia emerged from Wyatt's bedroom, a worried look on her face.

"He's still sleeping." She pulled the door shut behind her. "The dispatcher told me help is on the way. Officer Crenshaw, the one guarding our property last night, already called it in. He's at the fire."

"Good. Hopefully they'll get the fire out quickly." Cassie tugged her purse from the top shelf of the closet, where she knew Wyatt couldn't reach, and pulled out her weapon. She darted to the second-story window, wanting to inspect the fire.

She saw the fire, all right, blazing from this vantage point over the treetops, billowing thick, black smoke into the sky. She hoped the house wasn't a total loss, but more than that, she sent up a quick, fervent prayer, pleading for the safety of Eric and Seth as they raced toward the inferno. She watched as the truck slid to a stop, gravel from the driveway spraying, before Eric and Seth darted out of the vehicle and raced toward their parents' home.

She noted the horses trotting out to the pasture and felt a momentary flash of relief.

Then she saw a man, dressed in camo, creeping out of the woods, darting from tree to tree, hurriedly making his way closer to the house. He clutched a rifle.

Fear buzzed down Cassie's spine.

It *had* been a trap.

She gripped the Ruger tightly.

She had made a promise to Eric to keep his son safe, and she meant it. She unlatched the window lock.

When the man emerged from the woods, she slid the window up, took aim. More movement off to the side gave her pause. A second man in camo was also creeping through the woods.

The same pair who had chased them through town? Shot at them? The same duo who had shoved them into the river? Probably. Her anger flared. They could have hurt Wyatt, and they didn't have any reservations about hurting Eric.

She fired.

The gunshot reverberated, vibrated within her eardrums.

She heard Julia, whom she hadn't had time to warn, let out a shriek.

Wyatt wailed.

The man, the first one she'd spotted, the one closest to the house, whom she'd intentionally missed, spun and ran when the bark of the tree next to him splintered and flew through the air. She shot again.

Movement caught her attention, and she zeroed in on the other man. He was half-hidden behind a scraggly jack pine. She saw the barrel of his rifle peeking around the tree.

Cassie got off a shot before the man was able to. The ground near the base of the tree where he was standing exploded in a puff of dirt. In almost the same instant, the man fired, but in his surprise, he jerked the gun upward, and the shot blasted into the sky.

Cassie took another shot, not wanting to give him the chance to take aim again.

The second man whirled and took off running.

Though there was no doubt these men had nefarious intentions planned, she just couldn't bring herself to shoot them in the back as they fled. Shooting a running target in the leg from this distance, while they were dodging trees, was nearly impossible. They were far from innocent, she was sure, but did they deserve to die?

She couldn't make that call. They hadn't breached the ranch house. Wyatt was still safe, as long as she kept them at bay.

She would have to settle for scaring them, running them off and alerting the others to trouble.

As both men disappeared into the woods, she got off another shot.

Eric thought his heart would explode in his chest when a gunshot split the air. Then another…and another. All could be heard over the blaze. The officer on the scene stood with the garden hose his mother kept out. He wasn't making much headway, and he dropped the hose when the shots were fired, apparently realizing something other than the fire demanded attention.

Seth, who had been running toward the officer, whirled to face Eric.

"That came from the main house," Eric shouted.

"Go!" Seth pulled his keys from his pocket and tossed them to Eric.

Eric grabbed them midair and raced to his brother's truck.

In seconds he was tearing back down the driveway.

More than one gun had been fired. Had one of the shots come from Cassie? He hoped so.

His gut told him that the men who'd been chasing them down were the same men who'd started the fire. He realized that while the men wanted him alive, their paycheck depended on it, there was nothing keeping them from killing Cassie or his family.

He should have stayed behind. One look at the house close-up and it was clear it was going to be a total loss. Ella's pictures gone. The lock of hair from her first haircut, her blue ribbons from her track events, the jewelry box she'd made their mother in woodworking class in high school...all gone.

Leaving the ranch had been a futile move.

Had it been a deadly move?

He knew Cassie hadn't had her gun in the kitchen.

Eric was vaguely aware of the sound of sirens as he mentally berated himself. Cassie had warned that it was a trap. He hadn't disagreed, but he should have stayed at the house. Or let his dad go with Seth and remained near the house, letting the horses out of the barn. He had thought Cassie, Wyatt and his mom would be safe, barricaded inside the house.

Too late now, he thought, as Seth's truck bounced down the gravel driveway.

A camouflaged figure darted out in front of him. Eric hit the brakes, swerved. The man dived, rolled, slammed to the ground and then was up running again, back into the trees. Eric slapped a hand against the dashboard, frustrated that he'd been so taken by surprise he hadn't even been able to make out the man's features.

He was torn, feeling he should go after the man, but the greater desire to get back to the house won out.

Had that man infiltrated his home? He needed to know, so he gunned the engine again and raced back to his son.

As the ranch house came into view, he caught sight of his dad jogging up the front steps. At least one member of his family was safe.

The truck skidded to a stop, and in seconds he darted up the front porch. He flung the door open and found his father holding his mother close.

Cassie stood with Wyatt propped on her hip. His son looked shaken, tears shimmering in his eyes, but overall unharmed.

"Daddy," Wyatt said. "I wanted you."

The words were like a balm to his rattled soul.

"The gunshots scared him," Cassie said quietly, moving close to Eric, understanding he needed to hold his son himself. "He's all right, though."

Eric pulled both Cassie and Wyatt into his arms. He closed his eyes, held them close for a moment, as he thanked God for this answered prayer.

They were safe.

For now.

"Scared me, too," Eric said quietly. He released Cassie from his embrace, and Wyatt slid from her arms to his. His son rested his head on his shoulder. Despite the excitement, Wyatt wasn't used to being up at this hour and was still drowsy. "Scared me half to death. What happened?"

Cassie quickly told him what had gone down.

"That was quick thinking," Eric said. "Thank you."

"You'll have to replace the screen," Cassie said sheepishly.

"That's no matter," Eric said.

"The fire truck is here," James interjected.

Eric was glad to hear it, though he didn't have much hope for the structure. At least everyone was safe and the rest of the ranch would be spared.

It was nearly two hours later when Detective Mateo Bianchi showed up at the front door.

By then, the fire department had subdued the blaze. The fire chief had spoken briefly with James, letting him know that they'd discovered the melted remnants of what they assumed to be a gas can left on the front steps after the perimeter of the house was doused.

Eric invited the detective inside while Julia took Wyatt to the den to read a story. Seth and James were still down at the crime scene, speaking with the firefighters who'd stayed behind to be sure the fire didn't flare up again.

"Officer Crenshaw, the man we had staking out your place, caught one of the guys," he said without preamble. "A guy by the name of Dax Donaldson, from over in Red Lodge. He claims he was out deer hunting. Got lost and ended up on your property."

"Deer hunting?" Eric asked skeptically. "This time of year?"

"The sentence for poaching is less than the sentence for arson," the detective noted. "He surrendered without incident. Probably to play up the story that he was a nonthreat. Just a hunter lost in the woods."

"Lost? He wasn't that far from a main road," Cassie said.

"He sure wasn't," the detective agreed. "He tried to dispose of a smoke bomb as he ran. Another officer came across the canister and brought it in as evidence. He claimed he had it for protection." He paused, and Cassie had the uncanny notion he was trying not to roll his eyes. "In case he came across a bear."

"He was going to use a smoke bomb on a bear?" Eric scoffed.

"Mmm-hmm," the detective said through his clenched jaw, implying he wasn't buying this nonsense. "He also claims he had no idea there was at least one other man in the woods. He said he was coming up to the house to ask for directions when you shot at him."

"That's ridiculous," Cassie growled.

"I couldn't agree more," the detective replied. "My assumption is that he and his cohort were hoping to divide and conquer. Toss a smoke bomb through a window. Cause some chaos. They must have expected Eric to stay in the main house." He paused. "Or maybe they're after your boy. It would make sense he'd be left behind. You admitted you missed most of their conversation in the woods."

"But they did say they'd be skinned alive if they hurt Wyatt," Cassie reminded him.

"I can't help but wonder why that is. I suspect whoever is behind this killed Lorelei. Yet he wants Wyatt unharmed. Is that because he has some scruples about hurting a child? Or is there more to it than that?"

That thought hadn't escaped Eric, either.

"It makes me wonder exactly which one of you they are after." The detective looked grim. "I suspect they are after both of you."

"They're not going to get Wyatt," Eric grated out. "Lorelei told me to keep him safe. I don't know what she was running from, but she finally did something right by bringing him to me. I'll do whatever it takes to protect him."

"I have the perp's mug shot. Cassie, I need you to tell me if this is the man you described to me. The one who shot at you and Eric."

He brought up the photo, then tilted his phone toward Cassie.

Brow furrowed, she said, "No. That's not him."

He sighed. "I didn't think so. The man who shot up your business was bald. On the heftier side, you said. This guy doesn't look familiar at all? Could he be the other man that chased you through the woods?"

"It's definitely possible." Cassie studied the picture again. "But I can't positively ID him as the driver of the SUV. Or the man in the woods. I didn't get a good enough look."

Detective Bianchi showed the shot to Eric. "How about you? Do you recognize him? I'm not just talking from the other day. From anywhere."

Eric took a good look at the photo. The man was

thin. His eyes looked shadowed, his skin sallow. Half his face was covered by scruffy facial hair that matched the wild, overgrown hair sprouting from his head. The man had the sickly look to him that proclaimed an unhealthy lifestyle. Eric would guess drugs and alcohol were a big part of this man's routine.

He shook his head. "Like Cassie said, he could be one of the men who chased us through the woods. But I didn't have a clear enough view to say for sure, either."

"All right." The detective sounded disappointed but did not look surprised. "He does have a record. Theft. Drug possession. Assault outside a bar. I'd say he's the kind of guy looking for an easy buck."

"What happens now?"

"We'll hold him as long as we can." Detective Bianchi looked at Cassie. "I've been half expecting him to lawyer up. We already know from the conversation you overheard that he's been hired by someone, but so far, he's letting the court-appointed attorney represent him."

"I suppose it would be hard to sell the story that he was just a poacher if a fancy-pants attorney stepped in," Cassie mused.

"I'm hoping that if whoever hired him leaves him hanging long enough, he'll cave and start to talk. Until then—" The detective was cut off by the buzzing phone in his hand. He glanced at the screen. Frowning, he said, "I need to go. Something has come up with one of my other cases." He pivoted and headed toward the door. "I'll keep in touch," he said over his shoulder as he let himself out.

Feeling frustrated, Eric turned to Cassie. "I should feel better that they have someone in custody. But it's maddening that he won't talk."

"We need to head into town."

"*Now?* Cassie, someone just tried to burn my parents' home down. They pretty much succeeded," Eric reminded her.

"I'm well aware. That's exactly why now is a good time. Half the fire department is still on your property. Dax Donaldson is behind bars. I'm guessing the other man, whoever he is, will lie low for a while. That makes right now the perfect time to go talk to Sal."

He nodded, understanding where she was coming from. Before the detective arrived, Eric had given Cassie a rundown on everything he remembered from his time with Lorelei. Starting with when and where they'd met. Sal owned the diner where Lorelei had worked when she'd first come to town.

"I see your point. With so many people on the property, Wyatt would probably be safe here." Probably. But there was no guarantee. Still, Cassie was right. They needed to talk to Sal, and now seemed like the best time to do it. "If we leave soon, we should be able to catch Sal before the dinner rush."

Cassie nodded. "I'll grab my keys."

SEVEN

As Cassie parked across the street from the Good Stuff Café, Eric couldn't help but feel relieved they'd arrived without incident. Even though Dax was behind bars, at least one of their attackers still roamed free. And if they'd been hired by someone, did that mean with Dax incarcerated, they'd just hire someone else? Who had that kind of money?

The questions just kept piling up, while any answers were proving to be elusive. Maybe now, here, with Sal, they would catch a break.

"Ready?" Cassie gave his shoulder a squeeze.

"Yeah."

Lorelei had waitressed at the café. Eric, a bachelor and a worse-than-mediocre cook at the time, had eaten there on a regular basis. Lorelei had worked the dinner shift. They started chatting. Lorelei took her break and joined Eric for dinner a time or two. Eventually, he asked her out. She'd been hesitant at first, but she hadn't said no. They'd started dating. They'd gotten serious.

Or so he thought.

When it came to Lorelei, he wasn't sure of anything anymore.

The café door opened with a whoosh. He and Cassie

were greeted by the aroma of meat loaf and garlic mashed potatoes. The day's special, according to the chalkboard sign by the door. Just as they'd hoped, they had beaten the dinner rush. There were a few patrons seated, but most of the tables were empty.

A young waitress, probably still in her teens, approached them with a smile. "You can sit anywhere you'd like."

"Actually," Cassie said, taking charge, "we'd like to speak with Sal. Is he in?"

"He's in his office," Whitney, according to her name tag, said. "I'll go get him."

Cassie and Eric stood in front of the display case of pies, pretending to look them over.

"At least he's here," Cassie said.

"I just hope he remembers something," Eric replied.

"You said she worked here for nearly a year," she noted. "There's a good chance he'll have something to share."

Sal appeared, rounding the corner from the hallway that led to the restrooms, storage room and his office.

He flashed a polite smile. "Can I help you with something?"

"I hope so." Eric crossed the room to meet him and held out his hand in greeting. "I'm Eric Montgomery. I dated one of your employees, Lorelei Coffman, several years ago."

Sal's eyes lit up. Then he seemed to notice the somber tone of Eric's voice and he frowned. "Sure. Sure. I remember you. You used to come in for an evening meal. The two of you hit it off."

"That's right, sir," Eric said. "Would you have a few minutes to talk with us?"

Sal motioned toward a corner booth. He asked Whitney to bring three cups and a carafe of coffee.

Once they were seated and the coffee was poured, Eric broke the news of Lorelei's death to Sal.

"I hadn't heard," Sal said, sadness overtaking his features. "What a shame. What happened?" He reached toward the silver napkin holder that rested at the edge of the table. He tugged out a handful, blew his nose, then grabbed another handful to dab at his eyes.

"You two were close?" Cassie guessed.

He shook his head. "Not really, but I did have a soft spot for that girl."

Eric leaned across the table, keeping his voice low, not wanting to grab the attention of any of the diners. "She was murdered, Sal."

"No," he said in disbelief.

"Strangled, by the looks of it," Eric continued.

"Lorelei?" he asked mournfully, as if still trying to wrap his head around it. "Who would do such a thing?"

"There's an ongoing investigation," Eric said. "No one is hoping for answers more than I am."

"That's why we're here," Cassie interjected. "I'm a private investigator and a family friend. Eric hired me to help look into the case. Lorelei worked here when she first came to town." It wasn't a question, and she was all business now. "Can you tell me anything about that?"

"I don't doubt the two of you are on the up-and-up," Sal said. "Cassie, I know you've got a reputable business. We've attended a few of the same small-business owners' meetings in town. Eric, I remember when I figured out you and Lorelei were seeing each other. I was happy for her, relieved she'd found a good guy."

He sighed and looked at Cassie. "What do you want to know?"

Anything. And everything. Eric leaned back in the booth. It was time to keep his mouth shut and let Cassie do her job.

"I want to know whatever you can remember," Cassie replied. "No matter how small. It could be important. Did she ever talk about where she came from? Family? Old friends?"

"She didn't," Sal said. "She was a great waitress, good with the customers, but she kept things professional. She wasn't real big on chitchat."

"Can you start at the beginning, then?" Cassie suggested. "If you talk through it, you may remember more."

He nodded, glanced around the restaurant as if checking to be sure his customers were all doing okay. Apparently satisfied his staff had everything under control, he took a sip of coffee, glanced down at the table and then began to speak.

"I don't specifically remember the first time she came in," he began. "But I do recall she was in three, four times before asking me for a job. She always got coffee and a side order of wheat toast. I thought it was because she was a waif of a thing and that's all she needed to fill her up. Later, I decided that wasn't it. I can't offer my employees much by way of benefits, but one thing I've always offered is their meal at half price if it was purchased on their break. Lorelei never shied away from big meals and always finished her plate. I realized then that before I hired her, she'd been trying to stretch her pennies."

"How did you end up hiring her?" Cassie asked.

"Well now, like I said, it was probably the third or fourth time she came in. I'd had a help-wanted sign in the window for a while. I'd seen her studying it a few times. After she finished her breakfast one morning, she asked me for a job."

"Did you do any reference checks?"

Eric watched as the older man scrubbed a hand across his jaw. "Can't say that I did."

"Is that typical practice for you?" She kept her tone conversational rather than accusatory.

"No, Cassie, can't say that it is."

She let a few beats of silence hang in the air. Sal didn't seem interested in filling them.

"Is there a reason you didn't check?" she pressed.

"I suppose I should just tell you. No sense in dragging it out." The older man sighed. "When she asked me for the job, she also said she didn't need an hourly pay. She was happy working for tips. Before you ask," he said brusquely, "yes, I found that a bit strange. But you see, another thing I remember is that she always sat in that corner booth." He vaguely motioned to a booth that overlooked the street. "She was always looking out the window, but she was antsy. Almost jittery. I remember wondering if she was waiting for someone. Later, I decided it was more like she was on the lookout."

"Is that why you agreed to hire her without references and pay in tips only?" Cassie asked.

"In my defense, I want to say I've always run my business by the books. Always. But this one time, well, when I first told her no, she looked crushed. Desperate almost. To be honest, she begged for the job." He scrubbed his jaw again, as if needing to work himself up to going on. "Finally, she said she'd just gotten out of a bad situation. She was hiding from someone. She said she needed somewhere safe, where she couldn't be found. I decided then I had to help her. I knew I was bending the law just a bit, but I made a judgment call. I didn't regret it. Eventually she seemed to settle into life here. She stopped looking out the window all the time as if she expected to be ambushed."

The words hit Eric hard. "How did I never know this about her? She never told me she was running from someone."

"I s'pose you never had reason to ask," Sal said.

True, he thought, but shouldn't he have had a clue?

"It's not like she ever told me outright. I just assumed she was hiding from an ex. Some guy that had been rough with her," Sal continued.

Cassie sighed. "Unfortunately, that answers my next few questions. I was hoping you had employment records. A Social Security number and a driver's license. But if you paid her in tips, I don't suppose you do."

"You'd be supposing right," Sal said.

"Is there anything else you can remember?" Cassie asked. "Did she ever confide anything more to you? Did she ever talk about her past? Her family?"

He shook his head. "Like I said, she kept to herself."

"She had just moved to town," Cassie reminded him. "Did she ever talk about where she'd come from?"

Sal's brow furrowed, and it was clear he was trying to remember. After a few beats of silence, he shook his head. "It was four years ago. If she told me back then, I've forgotten it now."

Eric glanced at Cassie. She looked contemplative, as if trying to determine what to ask next. They had so little to go on.

"You know, there is one more thing," Sal said. "It's not much, and I don't know if it's of any use, but when she first came to town, she was living at the homeless shelter. I *do* remember that."

"Homeless shelter?" Eric echoed.

Sal nodded. "She didn't tell you that, either? I'm not surprised. It's not something she'd want to talk about."

"That's how she ended up living in your garage apartment?" Eric guessed.

"Even though she asked to work for tips only, I felt bad about it. She deserved more. I offered up the apartment. It was in rough shape. Hadn't been rented out in ages. But she cleaned it up, painted the walls and had it real respectable." He gave a half smile. "Honestly, knowing the little bit she shared about trying to stay off the grid, the wife and I felt better having her nearby. We wouldn't be great protection, but we were able to keep an eye out for her."

"Did you become close, then?" Cassie asked. "She worked for you. She lived on your property. Surely you had to have gotten to know her."

He shook his head. "I realized real quick she didn't like to talk about herself. So I quit asking. We talked about day-to-day stuff, but nothing of real importance. Still, I was as surprised as Eric here when she just up and disappeared. She left a note on the dinette table in the apartment thanking me for all I'd done for her." He shrugged. "And that was that. I'd hoped she'd moved on and created a good life for herself."

Cassie tapped her pen against her notepad.

"I guess that probably wasn't the case," Sal said. "You think her past caught up with her?"

"Yes," Cassie replied. "That's exactly what I think."

Eric could not agree more.

It soon became obvious that further questioning was futile. Sal seemed to want to help, but he simply didn't know much. When Cassie and Eric got up to leave, he took Cassie's business card and promised to call if he thought of anything else.

Once inside the vehicle, Eric noticed Cassie's gaze sweep their surroundings, and he felt comforted that she, too, was on the lookout.

"I don't know what to think. Sal said she seemed to be worried she was followed. But followed by an ex?"

"Maybe she double-crossed someone," Eric said.

"Maybe," Cassie muttered. "If that was the case, she's dead. They got their revenge. Why would they be after you? The men in the woods said their boss needed you to be able to talk. I understand Sal was going off limited information, but I don't think his assumption about an ex was accurate."

"And how does Wyatt fit into this?" Eric wanted to know. "I feel like the more we learn, the more questions I have."

Cassie told herself she was being paranoid, but she couldn't stop glancing in the rearview mirror. Eric noticed and swiveled his head, looking out the back.

"What is it?" he demanded.

Just then, the midsize white SUV turned on its blinker.

"That vehicle—the one that's turning now. It's followed us for several blocks. I thought it was tailing us. I guess I was wrong since they're turning off. They must have just been headed the same direction."

"Yeah, that's what I thought right before we got shoved into a river," Eric said. "Hope House is the next block up, but why don't you drive around the block first? See if the vehicle reappears."

"Better yet," Cassie said, turning on her blinker, "I'm going to double back." She did just that, taking a right, then taking another right, but the other vehicle was nowhere in sight.

"Feel better?"

"Not really," she admitted. Though the SUV was gone now, it had been keeping just far enough behind so as not to appear to be a tail, yet when she'd taken two unnecessary turns, the vehicle had done the same. She wondered if that was why it had turned off. Perhaps the driver had realized the turns were unnecessary, going off the main road, then coming back again. Perhaps they'd realized they'd been made and had decided to cut their losses and disappear.

"I don't, either," Eric admitted. "Let's get this over with so we can get back to the ranch. Maybe then I'll feel better."

A slight smile tipped her lips. "When you're back with Wyatt?"

"Yeah. It's funny how just being in the same room with him brings me peace."

Cassie pulled up to the curb in front of Hope House. It was a nondescript gray house with black shutters, encased by a white picket fence, on the edge of a residential neighborhood. A small sign hung by the front door, announcing they'd arrived at their destination.

"Maybe I should go in alone," Cassie said. "I know these types of establishments like to keep things low-key."

Eric shook his head. "I need to go with you. I need to see what the place is like. I can't believe Lorelei lived in a homeless shelter. The thought just doesn't mesh with the Lorelei I thought I knew."

"I have to be honest, Eric," Cassie said. "I don't think we're going to get much information. A resident's stay is confidential. But given the circumstances, we have nothing to lose."

They got out of the Cherokee. The sky was blue today, no sign of rain. But the early-spring wind had a bite to it. Cassie pulled her jacket a little tighter around herself. Eric opened the gate of the picket fence, allowing Cassie in first. When she glanced over her shoulder to thank him, she frowned.

"There goes that SUV again," she said as it drove through the intersection behind them. They *were* being followed. She knew it. Not much she could do about it now, though. She squinted, trying to get a look at the license plate. While the vehicle was pristine, the back plate appeared to have been smeared with mud, making it unreadable from this distance.

Eric twisted around, spotting it, too. "Let's get inside. It could be someone just dropped off a friend and they're headed home again, but I'm not up to taking chances these days."

Cassie wasn't, either. They hustled up the sidewalk. She knocked on the door. Then, when no one answered, she tried the knob. She wasn't sure what the protocol was for homeless shelters. It was locked, so she tried again.

A moment later, a petite woman with raven-black hair answered.

"Can I help you?" She had a polite but professional smile on her face.

"May we come in?" Cassie asked. "I promise not to

take much of your time, but we could really use your help."

The woman looked hesitant but allowed them entrance. They stepped into a foyer. Beige carpet covered the floor, and the walls were a comforting cream. A painting of a herd of mustangs hung over a worn-looking red sofa. A staircase rose right off the entryway. If there were any residents here now, they were out of sight.

"I'm Amelia Carrera, the director of Hope House. What is it that you think I can do for you?"

"We're wondering if you can tell us anything about this woman." Cassie held up her phone, displaying a photo of Lorelei that Eric had sent her. "She was a resident here several years ago."

Amelia frowned. "Are you law enforcement?"

"No," Eric said, "but she's the mother of my son. I have a few questions and—"

"I'm sorry." Amelia cut him off. "I only started here two years ago. Not that it matters. Rules are rules. I couldn't share any information with you, even if I wanted to."

"Please," Eric said. "My son's life could depend on it."

Amelia looked startled by Eric's proclamation, but she shook her head. Her tone was clipped when she said, "I can't help you. I'm afraid I'm going to have to ask you to leave."

"I understand," Cassie said. "I knew it was a long shot, but we had to try. I do have a question, though, and this I'm sure you can answer without breaking anyone's confidentiality."

Amelia lifted a brow.

"How far back do your records go? I realize you can't share specifics with me, but this woman, she went by Lorelei Coffman, would have been here about four or five years ago. Would you still have records?"

"We do," Amelia said hesitantly, as if now suspecting they may try to raid her files.

Cassie tugged a business card out of her purse. She held it out to Amelia. The woman took it with obvious reluctance.

"Thank you for your time." Cassie grabbed Eric by the shoulder. For just a moment, he hesitated, but she nodded toward the door and he complied.

Once outside, he said, "Cassie, we didn't try very hard. I can't believe you gave up, just like that."

Keeping an eye out for the SUV as they rushed back down the sidewalk, she said, "She wouldn't have talked. I've been interviewing people long enough to get a good read on people. I understand. She could lose her job if she did. However, now that we know the files still exist, I can let Detective Bianchi know. He can get a court order. It'll take a little longer, but he should be able to get the information, and we won't be putting anyone's job in jeopardy."

"I was just hoping for something," he admitted once inside the vehicle. "Sal didn't give us much to go on, and this lady gave us even less."

"Answers will come." Cassie tugged out her phone and texted a quick update to the detective, urging him to look into Lorelei's stay at the shelter. "We already know more than we knew this morning. We didn't know she lived in a homeless shelter, and we didn't know she worked for cash. It all goes right along with what Sal said. She was likely hiding from someone. And she has apparently been hiding from them for years."

Eric frowned and silence filled the vehicle.

Cassie found her thoughts floating back to the kiss. Had he done it on impulse, in the midst of an adrenaline rush? Or had kissing her been on his mind? Did he want to kiss her again? Or did he regret it?

Because, truth be told, she had wanted that kiss, had needed it.

They should talk about it, but it didn't seem like the appropriate time.

Or maybe she was just afraid of what his answer would be. She decided it was safer for her heart if she just pretended that quick, but lovely, kiss had never happened.

"Tell me, how did you end up taking over the ranch?" Cassie pulled away from the curb. It was a distraction tactic, but she also found herself wanting to know more than she should about Eric. "When we were younger, you had no interest in taking over. Your dad must be so happy."

"Yeah," Eric admitted, "he is. I almost missed my chance. A few years ago, he told me he was going to retire. I told him I still wasn't interested. Once he started selling off the herd, I guess it became a little more real to me. This ranch, it's my heritage. My legacy. Though I didn't know about Wyatt at the time, I couldn't help but think I'd regret not hanging on to it. It's a legacy I could pass down to my children, just like my dad and Grandpa Wyatt did."

"That was always your dad's dream. But I remember him saying he'd never force it on any of his kids. It had to be your dream, too."

He nodded. "Once he said they were putting the house up for sale, something clicked inside me. It became too final. I couldn't let him do it. I didn't mind my job, but I didn't love it. I missed riding out on Rio before sunrise, checking on fences. I missed a field full of calves. Mostly I missed the connection to God I felt as I spent the day working out in His great creation. Right around the time I decided to buy the ranch, Seth announced he was leaving the military and wanted to take up ranching as well. We had some long discussions on how we could make it work for both of us."

"Do you regret going into management?" She had heard that Eric ran the biggest sporting goods store in the area.

"I don't. I think God always makes sure we end up where we're supposed to be. Sometimes He has to slide the pieces around to make that happen. I wasn't ready to take over the ranch several years ago. My head wasn't in it, and I would've done a terrible job. Working as the manager of The Great Outdoors was a good experience. My time in management wasn't wasted. I've just readjusted my skill set now to make it appropriate for the ranch."

"The herd looks smaller than I remember," Cassie noted.

"It is. Like I said, Dad started selling off the cattle he had at the time. He was having a hard time finding reliable help. He couldn't manage on his own. When Seth and I decided to take over, we remembered Dad's motto. Work Smarter, Not Harder."

"How do you manage that on a ranch?" Cassie wondered.

"We switched to grass-fed beef. They bring in more money, but we had to reduce the herd size because of the pasture size. We don't supplement with corn or soy, so the pasture has to be enough to sustain the herd," he explained. "It's worked out well. With a smaller herd, we rarely have to bring in help, but we manage about the same profit. Dad is supposed to be retired, but he's not very good at it. He's out helping us most days."

"That would explain why I haven't seen any ranch hands." In years past, there had been other men on-site. She couldn't help but think that could provide a deterrent now, but that explained why she hadn't seen anyone.

"Right. Since we only hire guys from town a few times a year these days, Mom and Dad wanted to stay nearby to help out." He frowned. "That didn't work out too well for them."

"I know losing everything is devastating, but at least no one was hurt. They'll rebuild," Cassie assured him. "It must be nice to have Seth nearby, too."

"It is. I'm relieved to have him home. When he was overseas, I worried constantly about his safety. I prayed for him daily. I couldn't stand to lose another sibling."

"At least Nina stayed close to home."

"She didn't stray too far. She'll be home next month when she completes her program." A hint of a smile appeared. "I called her to tell her about Wyatt but told her now isn't a good time to come home. She's so excited to have a nephew. I can't wait for her to meet him."

Even though she had gotten Eric talking, *she* hadn't become distracted. Her gaze darted to the rearview mirror periodically. Though it didn't get close enough to cause a problem, she was sure she saw the white paint of an SUV flash in the distance.

Someone was keeping track of their whereabouts. The knowledge chilled her to her core.

EIGHT

Eric's heart cracked a little more every time he caught sight of his son's sad face. He'd told Wyatt his mother had gone to Heaven, explained it the best way he knew how, but he had no idea how much of it the three-year-old had grasped. At least Heaven and God hadn't been foreign concepts to him. Eric was grateful that Lorelei had attempted to instill faith in the boy.

When Eric found Wyatt standing in front of the picture window overlooking the pasture the next morning, his forehead pressed against the glass, he vowed to buy his son a swing set, a sandbox, a bicycle. And whatever else a young boy needed for outdoor play. He hated that his son, who clearly longed to be outdoors, had been locked inside for days on end.

"He needs to get out of this house," Julia said quietly as she came up behind Eric. "He's a child. He should be outside, enjoying the sunshine. Getting some fresh air. We need to get a swing set."

"I was just thinking that." Eric kept his voice low, hoping Wyatt wasn't paying attention. "As soon as this is over. He can't go outside right now." His mind conjured images of armed, camouflaged men creeping through the woods.

"I know it's not safe, so going out is not an option." Julia sighed. "But we've played every board game in the house. He needs something else to occupy his mind."

"Maybe we could take him to the barn," Cassie offered as she glanced up from the sofa, where she was working on her laptop. "It would be something different. I'm sure he'd enjoy seeing the horses."

"That's not a bad idea," Eric admitted. "A stray cat showed up here a few months ago. She had a litter of kittens out there. They're pretty active these days."

"Kittens?" Cassie asked, her tone almost reverential. She closed her laptop, placed it on the coffee table and rose to her feet. Her eyes glittered with interest, and the stress of the past few days seemed to melt away. "You have kittens in the barn and you are just now mentioning it?"

Eric chuckled. "Would you like to see them?"

"Most definitely," she admitted.

"How about you, little man?" Eric raised his voice a bit to get Wyatt's attention. "Would you like to make a trip to the barn? We have kittens."

Wyatt's eyes widened, and he nodded. "I like kittens."

"Me, too, kiddo. Me, too." Cassie ruffled his hair.

He smiled up at her, some of his sadness melting away.

"Seems your dad was holding out on us." Cassie winked. "But I guess that's okay because kittens are a really nice surprise. Don't you think?"

Wyatt's grin widened, and he nodded vigorously.

Eric's heart lightened at the sight of Cassie interacting with his child. He took a moment to just watch and listen as Cassie rattled off the names of Big Sky Ranch's horses for Wyatt.

After a moment, he glanced over at his mom, who had been awfully quiet. She wore a knowing look as she raised an eyebrow at him. He tried not to frown back at her. There was nothing to *know*. Cassie was here doing a job.

She wasn't here for *him*.

Sooner or later this whole ordeal would come to an end.

Then what?

Would they be friends?

Cassie would go back home. Would they go their separate ways and lose touch again?

Eric didn't like that thought at all.

He cleared his throat. "I'm going to do a quick perimeter check. Then we'll head to the barn."

Cassie nodded and took Wyatt's hand. "I'll help him get his shoes on while we wait."

After Eric thoroughly scoped out the woods from the second-floor windows, he hustled Cassie and Wyatt to the barn. The moment the doors closed behind them, they were greeted by the scent of hay and horses.

Rio, Eric's sleek black gelding, nickered from his stall.

Wyatt glanced up at Eric with curiosity.

"Can I touch him?" he asked in wonder.

"You sure can. How about I hold you up and introduce you?"

Wyatt nodded, and Eric scooped him into the crook of his arm.

"Have you ever been this close to a horse before?"

Wyatt shook his head. He reached tentatively toward Rio. The horse leaned his head into Wyatt's hand.

"Can I ride him?"

"Not today. But someday soon I'd like to take you for a ride. In fact, I'd like to get you a pony. I was right around your age when I started riding. What do you think about that?"

Wyatt's smile lit up his face.

Eric glanced around, looking for Cassie. He wasn't surprised to see her through the open stall door across from him. It was the empty stall the mama cat had helped herself to when she moved in.

"I'll introduce you to the other horses later," Eric told Wyatt. "Should we check out the kittens now?"

"Cassie found them," Wyatt said, pointing.

Eric stepped out of the stall and placed his son on his feet. Wyatt scurried over to Cassie.

She sat on a hay bale with a tiny, fluffy kitten held to her chest. She looked positively delighted.

"I always wanted a kitten." She glanced up at him. "But Mom was allergic. Deathly allergic, so it wasn't even an option. In high school I volunteered at the animal shelter."

"I didn't know that," Eric admitted.

"I was always grateful she didn't pass her allergy down to me," Cassie said with a rueful look. "Now I know why."

It was obvious that even though a few years had passed, Cassie was still hurt by her mother's betrayal. He wanted to say something, offer words of comfort, but he didn't know how to address the matter.

Instead, he said, "Why don't you have a cat now?"

She looked startled. "That's a very good question.

I've thought about getting a dog, but that's not real conducive to my sometimes erratic schedule. Cats are much more independent. That would be ideal. I think I'm going to have to remedy that situation."

Eric grinned and nodded toward the kitten she cuddled. "You can remedy it right now. You are more than welcome to take that little gal home with you."

Cassie's eyes lit up, causing Eric's heart to do a funny little swirl in his chest. She was so pretty, and there was such a natural glow about her. She seemed almost maternal, sitting there snuggling a kitten with Wyatt standing next to her, pressed into her side. He could all too easily picture the three of them together, fulfilling his desire for the family he'd often longed for. He couldn't help but wonder what Cassie would think if she could hear his thoughts. She clearly adored Wyatt, but Eric wasn't sure how she felt about him. Was she there simply to help? Or because her own home may not be safe at the moment? Was she there because Wyatt was Ella's nephew, and Cassie would've done anything for Ella?

He couldn't deny that his own feelings toward Cassie were growing, coming to life again with a vibrancy, with an intensity, he hadn't felt in years. Yet she'd given no indication whatsoever that she felt the same.

She'd been nothing but professional.

"May I really keep her?" she asked, pulling him from his reverie.

"What about me, Daddy?" Wyatt's lower lip trembled. "I want that kitten, too."

Eric knelt down to look his son in the eye. "There are two more kittens. How about we let Cassie have one? You can choose which one you want, and Uncle Seth said he'd like one for his barn. His horses need some help keeping the mice away."

"What about the mama?" Wyatt demanded, looking deeply concerned for her fate. Eric couldn't help but wonder if that was because the situation with his own mama was weighing heavily on him.

"Don't worry about her," Eric said comfortingly. "We're keeping her, and we'll take good care of her."

Wyatt tipped his head to the side. "What's her name?"

"That's a good question. I haven't given her one yet. Would you like to name her?"

Wyatt's eyes lit up, and he nodded. "Can we call her Patches?"

"Sounds perfect," Eric agreed "That's a great name for a calico."

"Wyatt," Cassie said softly, "would you like to name my kitten as well?"

"Cuddles," he said, without a moment's hesitation. "She loves cuddling you."

"Cuddles it is," Cassie agreed with a smile. "That's a lovely choice."

Wyatt then chose the orange tabby cat for himself, naming her Pumpkin. He designated the gray tabby cat for Seth and named him Meatball. Eric chuckled, wondering how Seth would feel about that. Then he realized Seth would probably like the name just fine.

"Can I hold one?" Wyatt wondered.

"Of course," Cassie said. She slid off the hay bale. "Have a seat because they can get kind of squirmy."

Wyatt wiggled himself onto the hay bale Cassie had just vacated. Kneeling in front of him, she handed him Pumpkin, his orange tabby.

"Be gentle," she urged. "They're pretty little, and even though they seem snuggly, you don't want to squeeze too hard."

"I won't."

The kitten melted into Wyatt's neck, causing his eyes to shine with delight. Eric could hear the tiny kitten's big purr from several feet away.

Cassie rose, then stepped out of the stall to stand next to him.

"This was good for Wyatt," she said. "He needed to do something normal."

"He actually looks happy."

Wyatt was completely absorbed in the kitten he was holding. Eric decided to take advantage of this rare quiet moment with Cassie.

"Soon there will be a lot more peaceful days like this," she said assuredly. "This rough patch is not going to last forever."

"Cassie, I've been thinking a lot about what's going to happen when this is over," Eric said, taking advantage of the lead-in she'd inadvertently provided.

"When this is over, the bad guys are going to prison. You'll build a relationship with your son. You'll build him a swing set, buy him a horse and catch up on everything you missed out on," she said quietly.

"That's all true. But what I meant is that I've been thinking about what's going to happen with us."

"Is there an us?" she asked, her tone curious.

He knew he wanted there to be. But did she?

He owed it to himself, and just maybe to Cassie as well, to put himself out there.

"The first night you stayed on the ranch, you said there had never been anything between us. But that wasn't exactly true. There *was* something between us. We just never had the opportunity to explore it. That was on me. And while I agree that there's no going back, what I want to know is if we can move forward." His tone was hopeful, and he took her hands in his.

"Move forward," she echoed with an unreadable expression.

He hesitated. There was a time when he'd known Cassie well. When he could read her expressions with ease. That was no longer the case. As he looked at her now, she seemed so guarded. He realized it was his fault she had put up a wall, and he had no idea how to begin to tear it down.

His resolve from just moments before started to crumble. Just because his feelings had begun to resurface, that didn't mean hers had. She had been nothing but professional, and he realized that she had given no indication of wanting anything other than a working relationship with him.

To be honest, he couldn't blame her. He should be happy she was still willing to speak to him.

He mentally began to backtrack, his original plan derailed.

"I hope we can be friends," he said.

Her eyebrow quirked, but her tone was flat when she repeated, "Friends?"

Cassie's cell phone chimed in her jacket pocket, saving him from having to elaborate. She gently pulled her hands from his. "I should see who it is. It could be important. It could be related to Lorelei's case."

She glanced at the screen and tilted it for Eric to see.

"Hope House? I left my card with Amelia. Maybe she changed her mind," she said expectantly. She answered the phone and was met with a moment of silence.

He wondered if she'd waited too long to take the call. Had the moment of hesitation cost them answers?

"Hello," Cassie said again. "Is anyone there?"

Finally, a soft, quiet voice said, "Ms. Anderson?"

"Yes, this is Cassie Anderson."

"The private investigator?"

"Yes," Cassie confirmed. "Who is this?"

Eric realized it was not Amelia. Amelia had been confident, outgoing. This person sounded as if they were cowering in a corner somewhere.

"You don't know me. My name is Mona Davenport. I…" She paused, pulled in a breath and continued. "I live at Hope House. On and off, I mean. I didn't mean to overhear your conversation yesterday. But I did."

"Go on," Cassie said, her tone casual. "I have Eric with me. You're on speakerphone."

Eric leaned forward, afraid of missing something.

"I know you were asking about Lorelei Coffman. I remember her. She was petite. Chestnut hair, blue eyes, with a beauty mark near her temple."

"Yes, that was her," Cassie said.

Eric's body seemed to be humming with anticipation. Were they finally going to get somewhere with this case?

"She was kind to me. When she left, she gave me some of her tip money to help me out," Mona said, her tone still hushed.

"What else can you tell me?" Cassie turned up the volume on her phone.

"I could probably tell you a lot of things," Mona replied, her voice louder now, thanks to the adjustment Cassie had made.

"What kind of things?"

"We were friends. But—"

Her sentence was cut off. Eric waited a moment for her to revive the conversation before saying, "Mona? Are you there?"

"I have to go," she said, her tone breathless. "This was a bad idea. We're not supposed to be using this phone."

"Wait!" Cassie interjected. "Mona, please!"

But it was too late. The other woman had disconnected.

"I can't believe she just hung up!" Eric growled. "Our first real lead and she just hung up!"

"You have a lead?" Julia asked as she entered the barn. Her curious gaze swung from Eric to Cassie. "I brought out some crumbled burger for the cat, saw you were on the phone and didn't want to interrupt. What kind of lead?"

"Someone who knew Lorelei while she lived at Hope House." Cassie fidgeted with her phone, brought up the number and attempted to call it back. No one answered.

"What did she say?" Julia asked.

"Not much," Eric grumped. "She hung up."

"Why?" Julia demanded.

"Apparently they aren't supposed to use the phone." Cassie waved her hand. "It's probably a security issue." She turned to Eric. "We have to go there. We need to try to catch her."

"I can't just leave," Eric said, his gaze instinctively sliding to Wyatt.

"You can," Julia said. "I'll get Wyatt back inside. Your dad and brother are out riding the fence line. I don't think they'll be gone much longer. I'll lock the door, keep the rifle within my sight, and we still have an officer keeping watch. We'll be fine."

Eric grimaced and scrubbed the back of his neck, clearly not comfortable with the idea.

"I can go alone," Cassie said quickly, and Eric knew she would without hesitation. "It's not a problem. I question people all the time." She headed toward the door. "I don't want to dawdle. She might take off. Or she might decide calling was a mistake if we wait too long."

When she turned around, Eric was right behind her. "I can't let you go alone." He had so many questions, he couldn't wait for answers. He turned to his mother. "Are you sure you'll be okay with Wyatt?"

"I'll set the alarm and lock the door," she said. "We'll be okay. If it will make you feel better, I'll call your father and brother and ask them to come in from the field."

He nodded. "I would feel better."

"Now that we've settled that," Cassie said, "let's not waste any more time."

Eric knocked impatiently on the front door of Hope House. This was the closest they'd come to an active lead, and he did not want to let it slip away.

He had no doubt they were being watched on the surveillance camera. The door finally swung open when it became clear that he and Cassie were not going to go away.

"You two again?" Amelia frowned. She stood in the doorway, her hand gripping the side of the door so they couldn't enter. "I told you yesterday, there are rules and regulations. Not to mention I respect my clients' privacy. I can't help you." Yesterday, she had been businesslike but polite. Today, she was clearly annoyed.

"We didn't come to see you," Cassie said quickly. "We received a phone call from one of your residents. She called from a Hope House line. She overheard us talking to you yesterday. She knew Lorelei. But we got disconnected." That was sort of the truth. The call had ended when Mona disconnected before Cassie and Eric were done speaking with her.

"We're looking for Mona Davenport," Eric said.

"I'm sorry. I can't help you." She began to swing the door shut, but Cassie put her hiking-boot-clad foot in the threshold.

"Please," Cassie implored. "Hear us out."

"The woman we're inquiring about, Lorelei Coffman, was murdered. Maybe you read the article on the front page of the paper?" Eric questioned. "The paper called her Jane Doe. I, and others in town, knew her as Lorelei. The other day, someone chased me down while I was with our son. He's only three. I'm scared to death he's going to be hurt in all of this, to be honest," Eric admitted, his tone full of feeling. "Then my parents' house was set ablaze. I'm hoping if we can figure out who Lorelei really was, we can figure out who is after me and my family."

Amelia's gaze darted between Cassie and Eric. A questioning furrow marred her brow, as if she wasn't quite sure if she should believe Eric.

"It's true," Cassie said. "Every word of it. I know you aren't able to share anything, but we received a phone call from Mona Davenport."

Amelia sighed. "There is no Mona Davenport."

"I know you have rules about confidentiality," Cassie pressed, "but we really need to speak to her. If you could just let her know we're here."

"I'm not protecting anyone. We really have no one here by that name." Amelia glanced over her shoulder, as if worried she would be caught divulging information. "Besides, we don't have an actual phone line. Each of our staff is assigned a cell phone. But we don't have a Hope House line. All emergency calls and inquiries come in on the line assigned to me," she said. "Residents don't have access to our phones."

"But the call said Hope House." Cassie held up her phone so Amelia could see the call marked Received.

The woman's frown deepened. "I don't recognize that number. I assure you, that call did not come from Hope House. Nor did it come from any of our residents. All of our lines are private. I am truly sorry about everything you've been through, but I honestly cannot help you."

A chill skittered down Eric's spine. If it hadn't come from Hope House, where had it come from?

Cassie had to have been thinking the same thing.

"Eric," she said, her tone laced with fear. "A person can change their display name. They can choose what others see on caller ID. They can choose anything, with no basis for it at all."

She put a hand on his shoulder and shoved him toward the porch steps. "We need to go. I have a very bad feeling about this."

A bad feeling?

Oh, yes, so did he.

Someone had conned them.

They'd fallen for it.

As they raced out of Hope House and leaped into the Cherokee, he prayed that Wyatt wasn't the one who ended up paying.

Cassie's heart pounded as she tore away from the curb.

With everything going on, why had they taken that call at face value? She should have realized that a place like Hope House would use a private number. Should have remembered that you could choose just about any name as your display name.

It would be easy to get her cell phone number. Anyone could find her business listing on the internet. Anyone who was trailing them, anyone with a shred of common sense, would realize they must be investigating Lorelei if they went to Hope House.

But she hadn't thought of that.

She had been so flustered by Eric's words, his suggestion that they be *friends*, that she apparently hadn't given her full attention to the phone call. She had thought he was going to suggest something...*more*. When he didn't, she felt disappointed and a little off-kilter. Her thoughts were left whirling.

Being friends with Eric wouldn't do. Eventually he would start dating again. He would marry. Some other woman would become Wyatt's mother, free to love on him and dote on him. And what was Cassie to do? Stand to the side and be his pal? His buddy? The very thought made her heart ache.

When Wyatt had snuggled into her side, she had wanted to wrap her arms around him and hold him close. The child had become precious to her in such a short amount of time.

No, being friends with Eric would be too painful. The thought of it rattled her.

They'd been lured away from the ranch because she had not been able to think clearly.

She groaned. "The vehicle yesterday, the one I thought was following us? I think they had something to do with this. They drove by when we were going into the shelter yesterday. They had to have known we were looking for answers regarding Lorelei."

"Where's the SUV today?" Eric wondered. "If they aren't following us—"

He broke off, his mind jumping to the worst-case scenario. Cassie wished her mind hadn't gone there as well.

"I need to check on Wyatt," Eric said. "If they wanted us away from the ranch..."

He couldn't even finish the thought, but he didn't have to. Cassie knew exactly what he was thinking.

Eric let out a growl of frustration. "I don't have my phone. We left in such a hurry I left it charging on the kitchen counter."

"Use mine." Cassie tugged her phone from her pocket and handed it over.

Her heart clenched as Eric tried calling his mother. She could hear the phone ring and ring. When it went to voice mail, he sent a text asking her to call immediately.

"I'm going to try Dad."

But before he could dial James, Cassie's phone rang. He hit Speakerphone.

"Eric." Julia sounded frantic and out of breath. "Wyatt's gone."

"Gone?" Eric snapped. "What do you mean gone? How could he be gone?"

"An officer came to the door." Julia moaned. "At least, I thought it was an officer. I let her in. But she... she shot me with a dart. I don't remember much after that. I passed out. Your call right now, the one I missed, must have awakened me. I didn't get to it in time. I shouted for Wyatt, but he's not here."

An officer? No. Oh, no. It wasn't an officer at the door. Someone had to have been posing as an officer.

That begged the question, what had happened to the real officer? Officer Crenshaw had been stationed at the end of the driveway when they'd left. Surely he wouldn't have willingly let someone pass.

Please let him be unharmed. Cassie sent up a silent prayer for the officer who had captured the gunman in the woods. She hoped the kidnapper hadn't used anything stronger than a dart on the cop.

"Mom." Eric cut into her slurred rambling.

Cassie's heart ached for her. Was she all right? What had she been drugged with? But Wyatt was their top concern. They needed answers, and they needed them fast. Cassie gripped the steering wheel, pressed the gas pedal a little harder as she turned onto the gravel country road that would lead them back to the ranch, but they were still miles away.

"Where's Wyatt?" Eric demanded. "Are you sure he's not there with you?"

Julia's voice broke on a sob. "I think she took him."

"Eric," Cassie said, her voice low but firm.

He glanced at her. She pointed out the windshield. An SUV was barreling toward them, heading away from the ranch. The road leading to the ranch didn't see much traffic. The vehicle was traveling fast, if the plume of dust trailing out behind it was any indication.

"What was the lady driving, Mom?" he asked insistently. "Did you see the vehicle?"

"A white SUV. One of those smaller ones that the sheriff's department has. Or at least, that's what I thought it was. I noticed it wasn't marked." She moaned again. "But you know, sometimes they do that."

Julia sounded miserable. Utterly heartbroken.

But she may have just given them a piece of crucial information. The vehicle that had been following them yesterday had been a small, white SUV.

The vehicle heading at them, right this moment, was also a compact SUV.

"Eric," Julia said, "there's something you should know. The woman, she—"

But Cassie didn't hear what she said. She slammed on the brakes, sending the Cherokee fishtailing. Eric's hands slammed onto the dash. He grunted in pain as his gash from the other day strained against the impact of his weight. Her phone went flying. He braced himself as she did an impressive three-point turn on the narrow road. Then, in a matter of seconds, they were racing after the woman who had just kidnapped Eric's son.

NINE

They tore down the gravel road, following the SUV through the thick curtain of dust that spewed out behind it. Fields of green gave way to a thin forest that seemed to thicken by the mile, but still Cassie wasn't able to close the distance between them.

"Where is the phone? I know Mom is calling this in, but I need to call Detective Bianchi."

Eric rummaged around to no avail. He wondered what had happened to the officer at the end of the driveway, but didn't ponder it too long. He was too concerned about his child.

"That has to be her." Cassie flicked a quick glance his way. "No one drives that fast on this road. There was a woman behind the wheel. She had sunglasses on, but I saw long dark hair. It's the same SUV that followed us yesterday—I'm sure."

"She had better slow down if she has my son in that vehicle. She's driving like a maniac," Eric grated out.

The woman hadn't slowed down at all. Now that Cassie was on her tail, she was speeding up.

Cassie let out a growl of frustration. "I don't want to hang back. But I'm afraid if I get too close, she'll drive so recklessly she'll go off the road. I can't take the chance that she'll crash or roll."

Eric knew what she meant. She wasn't risking it with Wyatt in the vehicle.

"Just don't lose her," he commanded.

"She's slowed down," Cassie said. "Not so slow that I can actually catch her, but at least she's driving somewhat reasonably now."

They followed behind the vehicle at a steady pace for several miles. When Cassie sped up, the woman did as well.

"This is ridiculous. Does she think she's going to get away from us?" Eric glanced at the dashboard. "You have a full tank of gas. We could keep this up for hours."

"I have no idea what she's thinking," Cassie admitted, completely baffled. "I'm certainly not going to let her out of my sight."

After several miles, the SUV's brake lights flickered. Then the vehicle took a sharp right onto a rutted dirt road. Cassie easily followed. Less than a mile down, the vehicle turned again. This time, there was a mailbox denoting a residence.

Cassie and Eric looked at each other.

"It could be another trap," Cassie warned.

"She has my son. That's a chance I'll have to take," Eric said. "But you don't. You can drop me off here. I can sneak through the woods—"

"No," Cassie said, not even entertaining the suggestion. "We're in this together."

They wove around a curve in the bumpy, muddy driveway, then came to an abrupt halt. The SUV had stopped in front of a cute, quaint cabin.

A woman had gotten out of the vehicle. She had her

back to them as she worked at getting Wyatt out of the rear seat.

Eric leaped from the still-moving Cherokee just as the woman pulled Wyatt free. She slammed the door shut and took off toward the cabin.

"Stop!" he ordered.

Wyatt spotted him over the woman's shoulder, and his face lit up.

"Daddy!"

Eric's heart skittered in relief. His son was unharmed, even if he was in the arms of a woman who was clearly unhinged. Why didn't she just give up? Surely she didn't think she'd get away with this now, did she?

For just a moment, he expected bullets to start flying, an attack to come from the woods, *something* in an effort to stop his and Cassie's approach.

He lunged at the woman, grabbed the arm that wasn't holding Wyatt.

She stumbled to a stop. Her thick curtain of chestnut hair covered her face. Then she twisted sideways, and he met her gaze head-on.

Those midnight blue eyes were so familiar.

Lorelei?

Eric sucked in a startled gasp. Without meaning to, he took a step back. His heart skipped a few beats, and his legs felt limp. Blinking in surprise, he tried to clear his vision, tried to clear his head.

He tried to make sense of the situation. Because his mind was telling him that what he was seeing simply wasn't possible.

Lorelei was dead. Her body was in the morgue. Cold. Lifeless. Her soul gone from this world. He had seen her himself. He had identified the body. How could this be?

Her eyes bored into his.

Eric realized then this wasn't Lorelei. But, oh, how she looked like her. Yet this woman had sharper cheekbones, fuller lips, and she tilted her chin in a defiant way Lorelei never had.

"Give me my son," Eric ground out, trying to keep his voice from shaking. He didn't want to give away how rattled he felt.

Without giving the woman a chance to respond, he tugged Wyatt from her arms, fully expecting her to protest.

She did not.

"Wyatt, sweetie, are you okay?" Cassie asked as she jogged up next to them.

He nodded emphatically. "I'm okay. I went for a ride with Aunt Frankie."

"Aunt Frankie?" Eric echoed. This woman was Lorelei's sister. She had to be. The resemblance was uncanny. Was this what his mother had started to warn him about before the phone flew out of his grip?

He was not surprised to realize he didn't know that Lorelei had a sister. She had lied to him about that, too. Not only had she told him she grew up in foster care, but she'd told him she was an only child. Was there ever going to be an end to the growing collection of lies?

"This woman is your aunt?" Cassie sounded somewhat incredulous.

Wyatt nodded and the woman frowned, as if irritated Wyatt had given away her identity. That was obviously not part of her plan.

Though he couldn't fathom what her plan actually was, other than absconding with his child.

"You're Lorelei's sister?" Cassie demanded. "Well, not Lorelei. But Wyatt's mother's sister?"

Frankie's brows hitched. Her voice was smooth as velvet when she spoke. "Figured that out, did you? That Lorelei's not her real name?"

"What *is* her real name?" Eric demanded.

"Not in front of little ears," Frankie said, her tone scolding as her gaze flickered to Wyatt.

Eric tried not to grimace. As much as he hated to admit it, she was probably right. He did not appreciate that this stranger seemed to have the parenting thing down more thoroughly than he did.

The woman's eyes darted around, but not in expectation. Fear? Yes, if Eric had to guess, she seemed nervous. Almost afraid, and despite the fact that he and Cassie had just chased her down after she'd kidnapped his son, she didn't seem to be afraid of *him*.

That struck him as incredibly odd. What, or who, was she afraid of, then?

"We should go inside," she said.

Cassie didn't budge. "You followed us yesterday, saw that we went to Hope House. You called my phone today and pretended to be Mona to get us out of the house."

Frankie shrugged. "Yes, I followed you. It was easy to guess what you were doing at Hope House. There's no point in denying it." She glanced around again. "I'm not discussing this here, out in the open."

Eric was about to protest. He wanted answers here. Now. *Right this second.* He didn't want to go inside. Didn't want to follow this woman's commands. But when she whirled and let herself into the cabin, he and Cassie shared a frustrated look, and he felt they had to follow.

Eric didn't doubt that she was Wyatt's aunt. She looked so similar to Lorelei it was almost mind-boggling, but did that mean they were safe with her? This woman had stolen Wyatt right out of his home.

She had knocked out his mother and had undoubtedly somehow managed to take out the officer watching over the ranch.

Then again, he was *not* going to leave without finding out what was going on.

"Let's go. I've got your back," Cassie whispered. Eric knew that was her subtle way of reminding him she was armed.

He stepped into the cabin, still holding Wyatt close. It was a cozy structure with an open floor plan. A small room in a back corner was the bathroom, most likely. Tucked into the nook beside it was a queen-size bed with a large suitcase resting on top. There was a small kitchenette and a sofa in front of a woodstove. It had the basic living essentials, and that was about it.

Somehow, he didn't think this place meshed with the vibe this woman gave off. Her flawless makeup and manicured nails screamed money. This cabin screamed rustic.

Her clothes, on the other hand, looked like they'd come from a costume shop. Which he was sure they did. It was a cheap police uniform, a fake, under close scrutiny. The material looked thin, the stitching shoddy and the badge clearly cheap plastic. But his mother wouldn't have had time to notice that.

Frankie crossed the room and plucked a tablet off

the table. "Wyatt, look, I brought you your favorite game. Would you like to play?"

He nodded, and Eric begrudgingly set his son down. Wyatt nestled onto the plaid couch, slid on his earphones and powered on the game. Clearly he'd done this before. Yet Eric found no comfort in the fact that Wyatt knew this woman, and that his son looked so content in such a volatile situation was disconcerting. But he was grateful, because the last thing he wanted was to cause Wyatt any more anxiety.

"You drugged my mother and kidnapped my child," he said, once his son was settled and unable to hear the conversation. "Why?"

Frankie tugged a hand through her shiny tresses. Even her hair looked expensive. The cut, the style, the highlights. They all implied wealth.

"It's a long story."

"We have time," Eric assured her. "Now get talking."

"You're right. The woman you know as Lorelei was my little sister," she said.

"Tell me her real name," Eric demanded before Cassie could.

She wasn't sure what to think of this woman. Having seen a few pictures of Lorelei, Cassie knew the family resemblance was clearly there. Wyatt trusted her, but could they? Not yet. She wasn't about to blindly trust this person, no matter who she was.

Frankie pulled in a shaky breath. "It's better that you don't know her name. Safer." She flicked a glance toward Wyatt. "Safer for all of you."

"*Safer?*" Eric scoffed. "You've been trying to kill

us. You had someone shoot at us, push us into a river, burn down—"

"No," she said vehemently, looking mortified at the thought. "That wasn't me. I never ran you off the road. I certainly didn't shoot at you. I've never even *held* a gun, let alone *shot* one. I'm trying to protect Wyatt from all of that."

"Who was it, then?" Cassie insisted, unable to keep the skepticism from her tone.

Frankie looked pained. Her gaze bounced between Cassie and Eric. "My father. *Our* father. He's a dangerous man. You don't want to cross him. The less you know about him, the better off you'll be."

Eric's eyes narrowed, and he darted a quick glance at Cassie. Understanding seemed to dawn on them both. The men in the woods had referred to the boss as *he* more than once. While it wasn't enough to put this woman in the clear, it did give credence to her story.

"That's who she had been running from all these years?" Eric asked forcefully. "Her own father?"

Frankie nodded.

Eric's gaze flicked to Wyatt. Then, satisfied he couldn't hear, he turned his attention back to Frankie.

"I assume you know your sister is dead." He gentled his tone. "She's been murdered."

Frankie squeezed her eyes shut, then nodded. "I know. That's why I need your help." She rushed on to say, her voice tremulous, "Our father had her killed."

The words seemed to hang in the air, almost too hard to grasp, as the horror of it echoed in the silence.

"You need to tell this to Detective Bianchi," Cassie finally told Frankie. "He needs to know."

The woman's eyes widened, and she shook her head

violently. "No. I can't get law enforcement involved. If I go to them, *he'll* know."

She didn't have to clarify that she was talking about her father. *Wyatt's grandfather*, Cassie realized with a jolt.

"He has eyes and ears everywhere," Frankie fretted. She seemed nervous. Jittery. Her eyes were wild, and she looked ready to bounce out of her own skin. "I can't let him find out I'm in town. He knew Lorelei was here, and I'm sure because of that he's already found a weak link in the department. Someone he could pay off. He had her killed, and if he knows I'm here, nosing around in what he thinks is his business, he'll kill me, too."

The waver in Frankie's voice almost caused Cassie to back down.

But it didn't.

"You can trust the detective." Cassie didn't know the detective well, but she knew in her heart that it was true. She had seen the compassion in his eyes, had heard the kindness in his tone when he assured them he would do everything possible to bring this case to a close. Cassie didn't believe for one second that the detective could be bought off. She trusted him completely. "He'll do whatever he can to help."

Frankie let out a sharp, nervous laugh. "He won't be able to do enough. You have no idea how powerful my father is. This Detective Bianchi, with this small-town department, is no match for someone as ruthless, as connected, as conniving as my father."

"If that's true, you need help from someone," Eric said. "And Cassie's right. You can trust him. I think you also need to explain to him how you impersonated an officer, assaulted an officer and assaulted my mother. You also kidnapped *my* son. No matter what you say about your father, you have to understand that, as far as we're concerned, you're far from innocent here."

"I did it for Wyatt." Frankie began to pace the short length of the cabin, making the structure feel even smaller. She clenched and unclenched her hands as she walked, as if she had so much nervous energy, she couldn't control it. "I was trying to keep him *safe*."

"You say that as if I should be grateful," Eric scoffed.

"You should be," Frankie admonished. "See how easily I took him? You should be grateful I got to him first."

"Did it ever occur to you to just warn us?" Cassie asked. "You could have sent an email, a text. You could have made a phone call. Clearly you have my number. You could have simply told us Wyatt was in danger."

Frankie blinked at Cassie in a way that said, no, that thought had never crossed her mind.

"I'm used to taking control of a situation," Frankie said. "I don't wait for others to do it for me."

Cassie felt as if the walls were closing in around them. This was taking too long, and she didn't like it. She wanted answers, and then she wanted to get out of here.

"You expect us to believe you kidnapped a child out of the goodness of your heart?" she scoffed.

"You don't understand," Frankie said, her tone almost a whisper.

When she quieted her tone like that, she sounded just like "Mona" had on the phone.

"Make us understand, then," Cassie ordered. The woman was right. There was so much they didn't know.

The answers she'd provided so far had only created more questions.

Frankie hesitated, looking to Wyatt for a long moment, as if his presence helped to calm her inner turmoil. She seemed to gather some resolve before returning her attention to Cassie and Eric.

"Our mother died in a car accident when we were young. Our father, probably to try to make up for our loss, spoiled us. We wanted for nothing. But he wasn't a very loving man. He worked a lot. Weeks on end would go by and we wouldn't see him. We were raised by nannies, then later, boarding school."

Eric rubbed his forehead.

Cassie imagined he was trying to reconcile that lifestyle with the knowledge that the same woman had lived in a homeless shelter.

"It wasn't until we were older that we began to question where his fortune came from," she continued. "Lorelei—I'm going to call her that, because it's too dangerous for you to know more—overheard him one day. We were in college by then, home on winter break. He was talking to business associates. She realized that he was engaged in illegal business dealings. *Dangerous* business dealings. Lorelei was furious. She became obsessed with trying to figure out just what our father was up to. He found out and threatened her." Frankie stopped pacing and turned to Eric. "She went on the run. Somehow, eventually, she landed here, in Mulberry Creek. She found you, which was not planned and really complicated her life." Frankie paused. "But *he* found her. I warned her. I'm the reason she took off four years ago."

She went on to explain that while Lorelei had left home, Frankie'd stayed behind because she hadn't be-

lieved Lorelei at first. It wasn't until Lorelei had been
gone for a while that Frankie also realized their father
needed to be stopped.

"Lorelei was collecting information on him. Compiling evidence. That's why he's so furious. Lorelei and
Wyatt have been hiding out in Florida the last few years.
She contacted me several weeks ago, and I went down
there. She told me she was ready to turn our father
in, wanted me to stay with Wyatt while she met with
the authorities." Frankie's eyes looked haunted. "But
something spooked her, and she took off with Wyatt. I
think she knew something might happen to her, so she
brought him to you."

"Where's the evidence?" Cassie found herself be-
lieving Frankie, even if she didn't trust her.

"That's just it." Frankie turned to Eric. "I thought she
was leaving it with you."

He shook his head. "She didn't leave anything with
me." He scoffed. "I take that back. She did leave me
with a son I didn't know existed."

Frankie studied his face. "Are you sure? She told me
she made a copy of everything. Then she said something cryptic like *I'm bringing it to the place I thought
I found forever with Eric.*" She stared at him, as if willing him to produce the evidence right then and there.

Cassie turned to Eric.

"I don't know what that means," he said, clearly
baffled.

Frankie seemed to deflate before them. "I need that
evidence. Wyatt and I won't be safe until we have it.
We won't be safe until my father's behind bars."

"He'd hurt Wyatt?" Eric asked in disgust. "He's just
a child."

Frankie frowned. "No. You don't understand. He doesn't want to *hurt* Wyatt. He wants to *raise* him. That's why I took him from the ranch. I wanted to get to him before my father did." She pointed at herself. "Me? He wants me dead. Just like my sister. You see, that's why it's so important for me to get my hands on the evidence. The only way we'll ever be safe is if he's locked away."

"You *need* to talk to the detective," Cassie said. "He needs to know this. You have to come clean about who your father is. Being elusive isn't helping anyone."

"I told you, it's better, safer, if you don't know," Frankie argued. "You can't go to the police with this information. At least not yet. Give me a few days to get away. If you go now, he'll know I'm here. Please," she begged, her entreating gaze bouncing between them. "Give me some more time to find the evidence. If you don't, you might as well be signing my death warrant."

Cassie glanced at Eric. He looked as torn as she felt.

"We can't keep this from Detective Bianchi," Cassie said. "You committed a crime this afternoon. Several, actually. Your sister was murdered. What you're asking us to do, it's wrong."

"No." Frankie took a step away from them. She glanced around the cabin wildly, as if looking for an escape route other than the door Cassie was blocking. "He's ruthless. If you go to the cops, he'll know I was here."

"The department can offer you protection," Eric said.

Cassie was glad they were on the same page. She had worried that Eric would be taken in by her pleas.

But really, this woman was no innocent, despite what might have been good intentions.

"No!" Frankie shouted this time. "I can't. Why won't you listen to me? He'll find me for sure, if he hasn't already."

In that instant, the sound of glass shattering filled the cabin. Flames erupted in a *whoosh* as a Molotov cocktail flew through the window and landed on the braided rug. The fire was instantaneous. Heat radiated outward, the flames leaping higher in the air with each passing second. The structure was so small that it wouldn't take long for the entire place to be engulfed.

"He's found us!" Frankie shouted, her tone equal parts fear and accusation.

Cassie yanked the front door open in time to catch a glimpse of a man running down the driveway, then darting into the woods.

Wyatt let out a shriek as he tore off the earphones and tossed the tablet aside. He scrambled into a standing position on the couch. His eyes were wide and terrified as the fire leaped and danced.

Eric dived toward him, yanking him into his arms.

"Eric!" Cassie shouted. He clutched Wyatt but turned to her. She tossed her keys to him.

Then she took off after the man. His bald head seemed to be a beacon, calling to her. He had shot at them before, tried to light them on fire now. She no longer had qualms about shooting him, if it came to that.

Wyatt and Eric wouldn't be safe until this henchman was taken down.

TEN

As the flames exploded in every direction, Eric caught sight of Cassie darting out the door, Ruger in hand. Eric had no idea where her weapon had come from. It had probably been tucked into her waistband, hidden by her jacket.

"Be careful!" he shouted as she raced after the assailant. He wanted to run after her, but first, he needed to tend to Wyatt.

"Daddy!" Wyatt screamed. "You're burning!"

Eric glanced down and realized flames licked at his ankles, setting his right jeans leg ablaze. His heart clenched in his chest at the sight. Still holding Wyatt, hoisting him high in the crook of his injured arm, he grabbed a heavy sofa pillow and smacked at the flame to extinguish it. Grateful for the protection of his cowboy boots, he raced toward the door.

"It's okay, Wyatt," he soothed. His son had a death grip around his neck. As they exited the cabin to the safety of the outdoors, he said, "We'll be okay."

"Where's Cassie?" Wyatt's tone neared panic. His gaze darted around. "And Auntie Frankie?"

It was only then that he realized Frankie had already run out of the cabin. She tugged open the door of the

SUV and sped away as Eric jogged to Cassie's Cherokee. He was furious she was getting away, but he had
no way to stop her.

Had Frankie been right? Had her father found her already? Had he sent his hired man to try to kill them all?
Maybe he hadn't realized Wyatt was inside the cabin.

"Cassie got out," Eric said. "She'll be right back."

*Please, oh, please, Lord, let her be right back. Watch
over her. Keep her safe. Bring her back to me.*

There was a time, in the years after Ella died, when
he thought he would never pray again. He'd decided
it was a fruitless act because he'd begged the Lord to
spare Ella's life, and his prayers had gone unanswered.
But he'd come to understand that sparing Ella was not
God's will, and he accepted that.

Now praying came to him as easily as it ever had.
He would trust that God would put a hedge of protection around Cassie.

"Aunt Frankie?" Wyatt worried.

Eric twisted Wyatt around so he could see the back
end of Frankie's vehicle rounding a corner, tearing away
from the crime scene. "She's safe, too."

He tugged open the back door of the Cherokee and
buckled Wyatt in. Then he hopped in the driver's seat
and pulled the vehicle away from the burning structure.
Guilt and frustration slammed through him. What should
he do? He couldn't very well chase after Cassie. Couldn't
leave Wyatt behind, and he didn't have a weapon to defend them.

Eric did the only thing he could think of. He scoured
the vehicle until he found her phone, somehow wedged
between the driver's seat and the armrest. The black
case had blended in with the black upholstery. After

connecting with the 911 dispatcher, he stated his multiple emergencies. An attempted kidnapping. A burning building. A kidnapper and an arsonist, both on the run.

He felt for Frankie. He saw the fear in her eyes, the tremble of her hand. But he couldn't, *wouldn't*, cover for her. To do so, he felt, would be to cover up a crime. In kidnapping his son, she'd also assaulted an officer. And while she may have thought she had good intentions, what she had done was still wrong.

Though she had said she took Wyatt to protect him from her father, Eric hadn't had the chance to ask her exactly what that meant. Had she ever planned on giving Wyatt back to him? Or was she going to take him on the run the way Lorelei had? Eric had a hunch it was the latter and, again, was so very grateful that they had been able to track her down.

As he was explaining the directions as best he could remember to the dispatcher, Cassie appeared, darting out of the trees. His heart leaped as relief cascaded through him.

"They'll be able to see the smoke," he said into the phone, effectively ending the conversation. He'd given her all the information he had by then and he disconnected.

The phone and the dispatcher forgotten, he hopped out of the vehicle.

"I lost him!" Cassie grated out as she jogged up to him.

His heart seemed to lighten a little as his gaze scoured over her. Her blond hair was tangled, and a few twigs were lodged here and there. She looked beautiful to him. Safe and *alive*. Thank God she was alive.

"The woods are so thick. I was afraid if I kept going,

I wouldn't be able to find my way back. Maybe I should have kept going. Maybe I should have—"

"Coming back here was the right decision," Eric assured her. "It's possible he wasn't alone. He could've been leading you into a trap."

She scowled, glancing around. "Where did Wyatt's loving aunt go?"

"She skedaddled the second we got out the door." He scanned the property, feeling uneasy, and could see the flames flickering behind the windows. It seemed the entire inside of the cabin was engulfed. He wondered if the roof would cave in soon.

The woods here were thick, and a forest fire in this area could easily get out of control and be devastating.

"I think we should go, too," Eric said. "I already called the fire in, and I don't think it's safe to stay here. Aside from the fire, like you said, it's all too easy to be ambushed. There's nothing we can do about the cabin." He motioned to the vehicle, and they hustled inside. This time, he was behind the driver's seat. "The emergency crew can follow the smoke. I don't want to sit around here, waiting for the arsonist to come back."

"Where's my phone?" Cassie asked.

He tugged it out of his pocket as he drove down the bumpy, rutted drive. He gave her a questioning look as he handed it to her.

"I'm calling Detective Bianchi. I noted the address on the mailbox when we drove up to the cabin. I also memorized the license plate on her vehicle. I think that's information he'd like to have."

She placed the call and relayed everything that had transpired to the detective, who was relieved to hear from them. He was at the ranch speaking with Eric's parents about the abduction. He hadn't heard about the fire yet. He assured Cassie that both of Eric's parents and Officer Crenshaw were fine and that he would let them know Wyatt was safe.

When she disconnected, she said, "He's going to wait for us at the ranch."

Eric nodded. Of course, the detective would have questions. Finally, though there were still a lot of blanks, they were starting to get some answers.

She glanced down and gasped. "Eric! Your jeans! They're scorched."

"Yeah. I sort of caught on fire. Obviously I managed to get it out before it did any real damage."

"You were on *fire*?" she demanded, horrified. She pressed a hand against her heart, as if to stop it from beating out of her chest. "You didn't get burned? Are you sure? You're not just trying to act all tough, are you?"

The concern in her eyes made his heart jolt.

She may not be in love with him, but she certainly cared. That much was clear. And it was a start.

"I'm okay. I promise," he said gently. "My skin was protected by the leather of my cowboy boots."

She blew out an audible sigh of relief. "I'm glad. I hate the thought of anyone hurting you."

He let out a humorless chuckle, his eyes briefly locking with hers. "The feeling is mutual, Cassie. The thought of you getting hurt in this ordeal, it guts me. I couldn't bear it if something happened to you."

"I feel the same," she admitted. Then, as if she didn't want to dwell on it, she hurried to say, "What did you think of *her*? Do you think she's on the up-and-up?"

Eric knew she was referring to Frankie, of course,

but with Wyatt in the back seat, she was trying to be discreet.

"I don't know," he admitted. "On one hand, I feel I'm skeptical of everything right now. On the other hand, her explanation makes a lot of sense." He paused. "But more than that, my little guy clearly knew her. He seemed to like her. That means he had to have spent at least a fair amount of time with her. I don't think Lorelei would have done that if she didn't trust her."

Cassie nodded. "I think your assessment makes sense."

Eric cast a glance in the rearview mirror. Though no one was trailing them, the black smoke billowed into the sky ominously. In that moment he realized just how dangerous the situation had been. At the time, he'd been running on adrenaline. Now it hit him. He'd been on *fire*. While holding Wyatt. If the fire had spread any faster, they could have been trapped inside the cabin. If he hadn't seen the throw pillow on the sofa, his entire leg could have gone up in flames. And then—

His breath quaked in his chest. His body tingled with the realization that if not for the grace of God, they could have had a very different outcome. He sent up a heartfelt prayer thanking God for the protection he'd been provided. Wyatt, too. It all could have ended terribly.

And this wasn't over yet.

Cassie saw the front door of the ranch house fly open as they rounded the curve in the driveway. Julia hustled outside, looking slightly wobbly. James hurried out after her, grabbing her arm to steady her.

Detective Bianchi's unmarked navy blue sedan was parked next to James's truck.

As Eric came to a stop beside the detective's car, his mother rushed toward them.

Eric opened his door.

"He's okay? He's really okay?" Julia cried.

Cassie's heart went out to the woman as she got out of the vehicle and gave her a sympathetic smile over the hood. Julia's face was creased with worry, her eyes shimmering with tears. Her body seemed to tremble, possibly a side effect of the tranquilizer. She looked wrecked.

"He's okay." Eric slid his arms around his mom, hugging her tight.

"Are *you* okay?" Cassie asked Julia. Not only was the woman visibly shaken, but she'd been scared half to death and drugged.

"I'm fine." Julia waved her hand as if to whisk away any worries. Her gaze bounced between Cassie and Eric. "I'm sorry. I'm just so sorry. I was supposed to take care of Wyatt, but I lost him on my watch. I'm so angry with myself. I can't believe I fell for her act. I should have known better than to open the door. It's just that the officers have been coming to the house before their shifts every night to introduce themselves, I thought maybe there was an early shift change."

"Now, don't blame yourself," James said. "I should've stayed at the house. Seth and I found a calf who'd had a run-in with some barbed wire. It took both of us to get him untangled, so we didn't get back to the house as quickly as I thought we would."

Cassie opened the back passenger door to let Wyatt out. He looked somber as she unbuckled his seat belt.

The kiddo had been through a lot already and now the fire. The hits kept coming. She was just grateful that kids seemed to be so resilient.

When Cassie smiled at him, he gave her a shy smile back as he reached for her. She slid him out of the back seat. Of course he was old enough to stand on his own two feet, but after what he'd been through, she thought he could use an extra snuggle or two. Hoisting him on her hip, she walked around the vehicle with him. His arms tightened around her neck, and she couldn't stop herself from pressing a kiss to the top of his head.

She glanced at Eric. He was watching her with a thoughtful gaze.

"Oh, there he is." Julia breathed in relief, as if she hadn't believed Eric and had needed to see for herself that Wyatt was all right. She held her arms out to him.

He held on to Cassie for a moment longer, and she relished the sweet warmth of his small body. The acrid scent of smoke lingered on him, and Cassie's heart clenched as she thought of the horror that had almost occurred.

But they were okay, and God willing, they would stay that way.

Finally, he leaned away from Cassie and slid into Julia's arms. James automatically reached over to help his wife in her weakened state.

"The detective told us about the fire. What a miracle you got out," Julia said.

"Hello," Detective Bianchi called from the porch before descending the steps. "Mind if I speak with Cassie and Eric for a minute?"

Cassie wondered how long he'd been standing there. He seemed like a good guy. Despite his busy schedule, he probably understood the family needed some time together after the latest near catastrophe.

"I'll take Wyatt in and give him a bath," Julia said to Eric. "Then I'll find him a snack." She took off toward the house, holding her grandchild close as James guided her.

"Looks like trouble follows the two of you," Detective Bianchi said. "I just checked in on the fire. It sounds like they'll be able to get it under control before it spreads."

"That's good news," Cassie said. "Do you have any other information for us?"

He nodded. "The cabin belongs to a woman named Meredith Cooper. She's from over by Bozeman. It was her husband's hunting cabin. He passed away, and she couldn't bear to part with it just yet. She's been renting it out through one of those online vacation rental sites. I spoke with her briefly. She said she rents to hunters, snowmobilers, anyone who wants to get away from it all. I caught her at her grandson's baseball practice. She said she'd check her records and call me back with the name of the renter."

"Do you think she'll follow through?" Cassie asked.

He nodded. "She was pretty attached to the cabin, upset it burned down. She wants this person caught. I have no doubt she'll be cooperative."

"I suppose it's too soon for any information on Frankie," Eric said.

"I put a BOLO out on the vehicle." The detective glanced at Cassie. "Good work getting the license plate. That's a rental vehicle, so we're working on contacting the company to find who it was rented to. As you can guess, I have a lot of work to do when I get back to the office. I'm hoping once I hear back from Mrs.

Cooper and the car rental company, I can really dig into Frankie's identity."

"I have a question for you," Eric said. "How did Frankie get past the officer at the end of the driveway?"

Detective Bianchi scowled. "She showed up looking all prim and proper, wearing a flowery dress, a crucifix around her neck, toting a casserole dish. When the deputy got out of his cruiser to question her, she claimed she was a member of your church. She said she heard your family was going through some struggles, so she wanted to drop off a lasagna for you." Bianchi shook his head. "I guess she was a real sweet talker."

"I'm sure she was." Eric grimaced.

"He wasn't going to let her by, though. That's when, quick as you please, she pulled her hand out of her jacket pocket and shot him with a dart gun." He shook his head again. "He should have been more alert, but she really sold the church-member act, and she showed him the pan of lasagna. To top it off, we've been looking for a bald man. Not a young, pretty, put-together woman."

"I wouldn't be too hard on him," Eric said. "My mom was also fooled."

"Tell me more about your encounter with this woman at the cabin." Detective Bianchi pulled out a notebook. "I need to know everything."

After the detective left, Cassie realized she was ravenous and thought Eric and Wyatt must be, too. She helped herself to sandwich fixings in the fridge and made them all something to eat. Julia was resting, and James and Seth were keeping watch over the property, determined not to allow another intruder on-site.

Detective Bianchi let them know another car would be patrolling the area, in addition to the one stationed at the end of the driveway. The ranch had been breached too many times for anyone's liking.

Once they were done with their meal, Eric gave Wyatt a cookie to eat at the table while Cassie started dishes. Eric carried a stack of plates over to the counter.

"If you're willing to wash, I'll dry and put away," he said.

"Sure," she replied, though dishes weren't really on her mind. She glanced over her shoulder and decided Wyatt was preoccupied with plucking the raisins out of his dessert. She leaned close to Eric. "I have an idea. Let's ask Wyatt what Lorelei's name was."

Eric frowned. "I tried that. He told me her name was Mommy. More than once."

She looked thoughtful. "Let me try another approach. Do you mind?"

He motioned toward Wyatt, giving her permission.

"Wyatt," Cassie said, her tone gentle as she moved away from the sink, "did you and your mommy spend a lot of time with Aunt Frankie?"

He nodded. "Aunt Frankie has lots of games."

"Did you go to Frankie's house? Or did she go to yours?" Cassie asked casually.

"She came to see us. But she brought the games and she brought ice cream, too," Wyatt added.

Cassie knew Eric had already asked Wyatt if he knew where they lived. He said in a house, not an apartment, but he didn't know what town. They lived near a park, and they often went to church. They went out for breakfast after church at a doughnut shop that he couldn't remember the name of.

"I heard you used to get doughnuts after church," Cassie said.

Wyatt nodded, still diligently plucking the raisins from his cookie.

"Frankie said you lived in Florida. Did you ever go see the ocean?"

Wyatt nodded. "Mommy liked the ocean. She lived by the ocean when she was little."

Eric's head snapped up. "Did she? I didn't know that. Did she tell you anything else about when she was little?"

"She lived by a needle, too," he said. "Isn't that silly?"

"A needle?" Cassie muttered. Then, trying to keep her tone casual, she said, "Wyatt, do you mean the Space Needle?"

He shrugged and took a bite of his crumbling cookie.

She leaned back in her chair so as not to appear intimidating. "Sweetheart, what was your mommy's name?"

Wyatt's brow wrinkled at her seemingly redundant question. "Mommy."

Eric nodded, not surprised by the response as Cassie caught his eye for a moment. She gave him a look, silently pleading with him to be patient with her line of questioning.

"But did she have another name?" Cassie asked. "Do you know what Aunt Frankie called your mommy?"

"Gina," Wyatt said, his tone clear and unmistakable.

"Gina," Eric repeated in a near whisper.

Cassie's heart thudded in her chest. At long last, had they at least partially discovered Lorelei's identity?

"Do you know her last name?" Cassie asked.

Wyatt frowned and shook his head.

"That's okay," Cassie said softly. "But you're sure? Aunt Frankie called your mommy Gina?"

He nodded.

"Did she ever call her anything else?"

Wyatt's forehead scrunched up in thought. "She called her *little sister*. But only when she was cranky."

Cassie shot Eric a surprised glance.

"Cranky? Like when they were fighting?" Eric asked, his tone conversational.

Wyatt nodded.

"Did they fight a lot? Your mommy and Frankie, I mean?" he continued.

Wyatt shook his head. "No. Not a lot." His lip trembled, and he set the cookie down. "I miss my mommy."

Cassie's heart dipped. She hadn't wanted to make Wyatt sad, but the information he had just shared could be invaluable.

Eric scooped him into his arms, gave him a hug and whispered comforting words that Cassie couldn't quite make out.

Cassie blew out a breath. Little by little, the pieces were coming together, but she didn't know if they would have the big picture before it was too late.

"Can I have my bear, Daddy?" Wyatt asked with a sniffle.

"Of course. Let's go find him."

Before he left the kitchen, he cast a glance her way, his expression full of hope and surprise. She knew he didn't want to say anything in front of Wyatt, but they may have just received their biggest clues yet.

Cassie went to her phone. She texted the detective the latest nuggets of information. Lorelei's name was

Gina. There was a good chance she was originally from Seattle, or at least nearby.

Eric strode into the kitchen as she placed her phone back on the counter.

Cassie had been scooping up the discarded raisins but looked at Eric in surprise.

"That was fast."

"Mom was coming down the staircase. She said she'd take him to his room, find his bear and see if he'll settle in for a story." Eric stared out the window over the kitchen sink. "I can't believe you got Wyatt to talk like that."

"He had just lost his mom. Maybe he wasn't ready to talk before."

"Or maybe you simply have a way with him. It sounds like she was from the Seattle area. He had to be talking about the Space Needle. And Puget Sound, maybe the Pacific Ocean. Her name was Gina. Nothing seems to fit other than Lorelei. I don't know if I'll ever get used to thinking of her as Gina."

"Gina and Frankie," Cassie said, feeling the names out. "Daughters of a crime boss."

"A crime boss," Eric echoed, shaking his head in disbelief. "My child is the grandson of a crime boss. I know Frankie said it earlier, but I still don't think I've fully wrapped my head around it. A man so evil he'd kill his own daughter?"

Cassie felt a chill shimmy down her spine. If Frankie could be believed, that was true. A man that wicked had Eric in his sights. He had sent his henchman to try to burn the cabin down with everyone, including Wyatt, inside. Was he that desperate to keep the evidence hidden? Did he not care that Wyatt was inside? Or did he not know?

The thought was terrifying. Reflexively, she moved toward Eric, put her arms around him. He tensed in a moment of surprise, but then relaxed and held her close.

"He has to be stopped." He *had* to be stopped, before anyone else was hurt. As she stood here with Eric, she couldn't deny her feelings any longer. She had loved him once, vowed not to get close to him while working this assignment, but here she was…allowing him to steal her heart all over again.

She knew she shouldn't let that happen, but as they stood there, drawing on each other's strength, she felt unable to stop herself. Knowing that Eric could have been badly injured today in the fire resonated deep down in her soul.

She wasn't ready to lose him.

Not again.

"He will be stopped." Eric pressed a kiss to the top of her forehead. "Because there is no way I am going to let a monster like that raise my son."

ELEVEN

Seth and James had decided to take turns watching over the ranch while everyone slept. They were all a little leery of the arsonist after Eric's parents' house and the cabin both burned. No one wanted a Molotov cocktail to fly into the ranch house. Eric felt bad not taking a turn as well, but his dad and brother insisted that Eric had too much going on during the day to give up sleeping at night.

Unfortunately, they were right.

When he shuffled down the steps the following morning, he found his dad standing in the kitchen, gazing out the window and drinking a cup of coffee. James noticed Eric and he twisted around, leaning against the counter.

"Quiet night, I hope?" Eric wondered.

"It was. Seth's watch was quiet as well."

"Maybe you should go get some sleep," Eric suggested.

"Nah. Now that the sun is up, I'd never drift off."

Eric should have known better than to ask. After helping himself to a cup of coffee, he leaned against the counter, unconsciously mimicking his father. He glanced toward the door, half expecting Cassie to be down any minute. She seemed to be an early riser.

"Looking for your girl?"

Eric lowered his head and winced, embarrassed at having been so obvious. "Thing is, she's not my girl."

"But you want her to be. Don't deny it."

He couldn't deny it, wouldn't even try. Especially not after Cassie had stepped into his arms last night. She had taken him completely by surprise, yet holding her felt as natural as breathing. He wanted to be able to pull her to him, hold her close every day for the rest of his life.

"I thought years ago that something romantic was brewing between the two of you. Your mom saw it, too. Then nothing." His dad took a long, slow sip of the steaming liquid. "Actually, it seemed worse than nothing. You two have a secret romance that you kept from us all? Then a nasty breakup? I've always wondered what happened there but thought it was best not to pry."

Eric cocked an eyebrow. "But you changed your mind and you're prying now?"

His dad smirked, shrugged, took another sip of coffee. "Guess I am. Going to tell me what happened all those years ago?"

Eric didn't want to, but maybe it was time he came clean.

"I did something pretty awful," he began.

"I'm listening," James said, his tone calm and comforting.

"I blamed her for Ella's death."

His father was silent for a moment, as if not quite comprehending what Eric had said.

Eric sipped his coffee but couldn't look at his father.

"I'm trying to figure out how you could have come to that conclusion, even temporarily, but I'm stumped," James said. "Care to tell me about it?"

"At the time, I thought she should have done more to convince Ella to take the experimental treatment," Eric admitted. "They were so close, Ella and Cassie, I mean. I was sure that if Cassie had encouraged her to take it, she would have."

"Now, why would you think that?" James pressed. "Ella didn't listen to your mother or me when we asked her to. You and Ella were close as could be. She didn't take it at your urging, either. Why do you think Cassie could've made a difference?"

"I've spent a lot of time thinking about that over the years. I think I was mad that Cassie didn't even try. I was angry that Ella was sick, dying, and I was looking for someone to blame. So, I blamed her."

James cleared his throat. "I hope you've given her a proper apology."

Eric grimaced. "I can't say that I have."

"What are you waiting for?" James prodded.

"You're right. As soon as she gets up, we'll have a talk."

"Go have your talk now. Cassie is out in the barn. You just missed her. She said something about not sleeping well and needing some kitten therapy."

That was all the urging he needed. He gulped down the rest of his coffee, rinsed out his mug, then headed out to the barn.

He found Cassie there, perched on a hay bale, snuggling with Cuddles. The mama cat and the other two kittens rested near her feet. She glanced up when he walked in and flashed him a lazy smile.

"Their purring," she said as she scratched Cuddles between the ears, "is so relaxing. Did you know studies show that a cat's purr can cause bones to heal faster? People with cats have a reduced risk of stroke. Probably because their purring lowers blood pressure."

"Really?" Eric asked, slightly skeptical.

She shrugged. "I read it on the internet. I don't know if it's true, but I'm feeling calmer already."

She patted the hay bale across from her.

He dropped down onto it, and she promptly scooped up Meatball and handed him to Eric. The little gray tabby began purring like a champ. Eric couldn't help but smile as it helped itself to a spot on his lap and curled right up into a ball.

"See? I think you feel better already, too."

"You know what would make me feel better?" he asked, before he lost his nerve. "If I could get something off my chest. I should have done this years ago."

He glanced at Cassie. She was looking at Cuddles, but he could tell she was listening to him.

"I owe you an apology. A big one. The other day when we were out here, when I asked you if we could move forward, I should have started with that. I'm sorry. I should have told you that *years* ago. I wish I could take back every hurtful word I said. I know you loved Ella. I know you only wanted what was best for her."

"What hurt the most was that you would even question my love for her," she admitted quietly. Her tone emanated the years of pain she felt. "She was my best friend from kindergarten on. I don't think I'll ever have another friend like her. When she died, a part of me died with her. I didn't grow up with siblings, but I loved her like a sister."

"I know. That's why what I said was so awful."

Cassie glanced up at him, surprised to hear him say the words. She couldn't help but agree. "You were awful."

He winced. "I'm not that person anymore."

"Good, because I didn't like that person very much."

The night Ella died, Eric had followed Cassie out to the hospital parking lot. He had told her she acted as if she didn't care for Ella at all. Hadn't cared about what happened to her. Hadn't cared whether she lived or died.

"There were no guarantees with the experimental treatment, Eric. You knew that. By the time her oncologist mentioned it to her, she was already so sick, so worn down. So…weary of it all. With no guarantees, she didn't want to live the rest of her life that way. She wanted to enjoy the little time she had left. I didn't want to deny her that."

Ella had refused an experimental treatment that had horrible side effects and unproved results. Her family had begged her to take it. Ella, whose faith was as strong as anyone Cassie had ever known, hadn't wanted to prolong a miserable life on earth. Only months into her illness, her body had already begun giving out on her. Pain wreaked havoc on a daily basis, convincing her she was ready to be called home to her Lord.

Her family implored her to fight. Pleaded with her to take the experimental drug.

But Ella stood firm in her faith, in her desire to give in to her Heavenly reward. Only Cassie had supported her decision. No one would ever know how much it broke her heart, simply shattered her to do so, but she did it with Ella's wishes in mind.

Yet when Eric had accused her of letting Ella die, she had so much guilt, wondering if she had made the right decision after all.

"I know. I see that now. I should have thanked you for supporting her, standing by her," he acknowledged. "I was wrong. So terribly wrong. It was her choice to make. I made it difficult for her, when *I* should have been the one supporting her. I was lost in my own grief. I don't think I truly comprehended her pain. Both physical and emotional."

"It broke my heart, Eric. First, I lost her. Then I lost you." She winced. "Not that you and I ever had the chance to make it official. But I cared for you, a lot, long before the night we got trapped in the gazebo."

"I was grateful for that thunderstorm," Eric admitted, "because I'd had feelings for you for a long time, too. I'd been waiting for the right time to tell you."

Before they could explore their feelings further, before they could get Ella's blessing, Ella had made a staggering announcement. Though her family knew she'd been feeling under the weather, they hadn't realized how serious her symptoms had become. They hadn't known she'd been worried enough to seek out medical treatment. Her tearful announcement that she had just been diagnosed with an aggressive, terminal ovarian cancer had stunned them all.

She was only twenty-four. She had seemed healthy in every regard.

Up until she wasn't.

Any thought of romance between Eric and Cassie had been sidelined.

"I have a question for you," Eric said. "I know it's personal, and probably none of my business, but I'm going to ask it anyway."

She arched a brow at him.

"Why aren't you married? You're beautiful. Successful. You have the biggest heart of anyone I know."

She shrugged and looked at the kitten again.

"I was in a serious relationship when Mom died. His name was Aaron. At first, he was really supportive. Understanding. Patient." She winced. "That started to change after I found my adoption papers. I can't blame him entirely. I became pretty focused on finding my birth mother. He thought I was obsessed with it. He told me she'd given me up for a reason—I should respect that and let it go. That attitude drove a wedge between us. He didn't understand how alone I felt. I needed that connection. I needed answers. Not only from my birth mom, but I wanted insight into why Mom always kept it a secret."

"Did you get the answers you wanted?"

"For the most part. She gave me up because she was only seventeen. She said she was in love with my birth father, but that he led a troubled life. He died in a motorcycle accident before he knew about me."

"That part was true, then," Eric said. "Your mom, Maggie, I mean, told you your father died in a motorcycle accident."

"She did. She simply failed to mention that my father was a man she had never met. Whenever I would ask about him, she would get emotional and say she couldn't talk about it. I didn't want to hurt her, so I didn't bring him up often. Now I wonder if that was an easy way for her to shut down the conversation."

"Danae couldn't raise you on her own?"

"Her parents kicked her out of the house. She felt she had no choice." She sighed. "Deep down, I understand. But it was a lot to process. All she knew of my adoptive mother was that she couldn't have children—which was more than I ever knew—and desperately wanted a child."

"That's a lot to take in."

"It was. It still is. None of it explained why Mom kept it from me, though. I have to guess she was afraid it would change our relationship."

"The boyfriend didn't handle it well? You finding your birth mom?"

"Shortly after I connected with Danae, Aaron told me we should take a break. He suggested I needed to get my priorities straight and concentrate on him, since he was the one who'd been there for me." She snorted a humorless laugh. "We went our separate ways. He ended up accepting a job offer in Bozeman. I kind of wonder if that was really what instigated the breakup."

"You were abandoned again, when you needed support the most."

Cassie shrugged, wishing it was no big deal. But it was.

"After that, I decided that helping others find people was my calling. I've spent a lot of time and effort building my business, building a name for myself. I haven't had time to date."

Or maybe it had less to do with time and more to do with the fact that she was tired of being let down.

"What about now?"

She blinked at him, a look of confusion settling on her face. "What do you mean?"

"Do you have time to date now? I'm specifically wondering if you would have time to date me."

Cassie let his words hang in the air for a moment. She had loved Eric at one time. Had even thought he was the one God had chosen for her. She had been idealistic and foolish. He clearly had not been the one.

Or was he?

Was he the one God had chosen for her, and though it hadn't worked out the first time, were they being given a second chance?

The idea was startling and almost too much to grasp in that moment.

She knew she was falling in love with him.

Yet she wasn't prepared to give him her heart yet. The other day, when he'd mentioned being friends, she had thought she wanted more. Now she wasn't sure she was ready.

She had been hurt one too many times by the people closest to her.

"Eric, there's so much going on."

"We never got the opportunity to see where a relationship would go all those years ago, and that's on me. But maybe we've been given another chance."

She was surprised that his words so closely mirrored her thoughts. Still, she needed some time to process his apology.

"Until this is over, I don't think it's a good idea," she hedged, afraid of what giving her heart away again would mean.

"Why?" He sounded more curious than anything.

"Apparently I can't think clearly when I'm around you.

The day we got the call from Hope House, I should've realized the phone call was a possible hoax. I need to concentrate on this case. Until this is solved, I need a clear head. I shouldn't be thinking about anything else."

"And once this is over?" he pressed.

She bit her lip, remaining silent.

His lips quirked up, ever so slightly. "You aren't saying no."

She sighed. "Maybe I don't want to say no. I think I'm simply saying not yet."

He was quiet a moment, studying her. Then he stood, and she thought he was going to walk away.

Instead, he leaned down, cupped her cheek and placed a soft, sweet, gentle kiss to her lips. She was frozen in surprise for only a moment. Then what was left of her resolve melted away. She returned the kiss as a flood of emotions cascaded over her. She wanted Eric in a way she had never wanted anyone else.

She wanted a life with him. A family. A future.

He straightened. "I'm willing to wait. If you let me in, Cassie, I promise not to abandon you. Not ever again."

She sat there, reeling from the kiss. Reeling from the emotions that were whirling out of control. For so long, she had managed to box up her feelings for Eric, pack them away and keep them at bay.

But with one kiss, they had all come flooding forth.

As she sat there with the purring kitten in her lap, she looked Heavenward.

Lord, please guide me. If Eric is the one for me, please show me the way.

When Cassie came back in the house, Eric cast a quick glance at her, but she was checking her phone.

He couldn't believe he'd kissed her. Maybe he shouldn't have done that. She was right. He didn't want to admit it, but it would be best if they waited to sort out their feelings. There was already too much going on, too much at stake to allow their attention to be divided.

He needed to set his feelings aside.

For now.

He believed God had put her back in his life for a reason. There had been two other private investigators in the listings he searched. But C. J. Anderson was the one his intuition had told him he should go with. He knew now it wasn't just intuition but God whispering to his heart, leading him back to Cassie.

But now was not the time.

The family was barely seated when Eric's phone rang. Under normal circumstances, the family did not bring their phones to the dinner table. Things were far from normal right now.

Eric glanced at the screen. "It's the detective. I need to get this." He rose from the table, accepting the call. Cassie slid from her chair and followed after him. "Cassie's here," he told Detective Bianchi as they entered the privacy of the family room. "Is it okay if I put you on speakerphone?"

"Go ahead. It's because of the last bit of information that she sent along that I think we know who our Jane Doe, er, Lorelei is," Detective Bianchi said, apparently remembering Eric's request not to refer to her as Jane Doe. "There's a suspected crime boss based out of Seattle. His name's Tom McClellan. He owns a national chain of furniture stores, but that's most likely a front to hide where the real money is pouring in from. He appears to be a bit of a philanthropist, but he's on the ATF's radar for suspected arms dealing. It's likely he uses the trucking fleet that ships furniture to also ship the weapons."

"I've never heard of him," Eric observed.

"No reason you would have. He's just a high-level thug. One of too many to count across the country. Each year tens of thousands of weapons are smuggled into Mexico. Mostly handguns, but it's big business. He must be doing well at it because the man's a billionaire. Here's the thing. He has two daughters. Francesca, age twenty-nine, and Regina, twenty-seven. I've scoured the internet, but it appears security has been tight around these two. I'm guessing this man has enemies, so he tried to keep his daughters out of the public eye. Neither has a social media presence. No newspaper photos from any of the dozens of events he's attended and donated to."

"So, we can't confirm," Eric guessed.

"I didn't say that. I was able to pull copies of their driver's licenses from the DMV. I'd like to send them to you. Let me know what you think." He paused. "Eric, I know this isn't over yet, but if this pans out the way I think, this could be the break we need."

"I hope so."

"Me, too. I don't know how much of what Frankie told you was true. I don't know if there really is a packet of evidence, but if she's right…" He whistled. "It would be huge if we could bring this man down."

"It sounds like it."

"I'm going to send the pictures now. The first will be of Francesca. The second," he said, his tone softening just a bit, "will be of Regina."

Lorelei. The second photo would be of Lorelei.

In a matter of seconds, he was looking at the first photo. The woman in the picture was far more put-together than the one yesterday had been. Perfect makeup. Flawless hair. Diamonds glittering in her ears. As opposed to yesterday, when she'd been wearing a costume uniform. While she had emanated wealth, she had looked slightly frazzled after attempting to kidnap a child.

"That's her," he said. "That's Wyatt's aunt Frankie."

"Are you positive?"

"Absolutely," Eric said.

Cassie, who had been peering over his shoulder, nodded her agreement.

"I'll send the next picture now."

Eric braced himself, and in no time, he was looking into the much younger face of Lorelei. *No.* Regina. Regina McClellan. He wasn't prepared for the wave of emotion that slammed into him. She looked so young in the picture. He had to guess it was close to a decade old. She'd been on the run for some time.

"Yeah." His voice sounded strained. "That is, without a doubt, the woman I knew as Lorelei."

He suddenly saw the woman in a different light. He didn't think of her now as the woman who had disappeared, keeping his son from him. He viewed her now as the woman who had given her life trying to protect their son. The woman had, presumably, dedicated her life to trying to bring down her father, a man likely responsible for countless deaths.

"I was pretty certain it was her, but I'm relieved you're able to confirm that," Detective Bianchi said. "I have other information, too. I was able to get the records on the rental car and the hunting cabin."

"And?" Eric pressed when he felt the detective waited a few beats too long to divulge the information.

"According to the rental agreements, they were both paid for by Vanessa Walters."

Cassie and Eric shared a confused look.

"Vanessa Walters?" Cassie repeated.

"Someone else is involved in this?" Eric asked.

"I don't think so." The detective went on to explain that while investigating Vanessa Walters, he discovered the woman in question had died over two years ago. "However, her Social Security number was tied to the bank account used to pay for both the car and the cabin. Her driver's license was used for the rental car. The woman had the same coloring as Francesca. I don't think the clerks at these places look at the photos real closely."

"Are you saying Francesca stole this woman's identity?" Cassie asked.

"It sure looks like it," Detective Bianchi said. "If Regina had the connections to do so, it would only make sense her sister would as well. It sure does complicate matters, though. It's hard to track someone down when their identity keeps changing."

"You can say that again," Cassie muttered.

"I have one last bit of information," the detective continued. "The toxicology report just came in. Regina had traces of Rohypnol in her system. The drug would've subdued her, probably even knocked her out, so strangling her would've been easy for her killer."

"She never had a chance," Cassie said quietly.

"Eric, I don't mean to put the pressure on you, but if Regina left evidence, we could really use it. Not only could it bring this man down, but without it, I'm afraid he could get away with murder."

"There would be no motive," Cassie guessed.

"Correct," the detective said. "He's worked hard to build a positive reputation for himself, giving substantial sums to different charities. It would be hard to convince a jury that he had his own child killed."

Eric's heart stuttered. Not only would the man get away with murder, but he would be free to come after Wyatt over and over again.

Eric had to figure out where that evidence was.

Please, Lord, help me to understand Lorelei's clue.

TWELVE

As Eric bounded down the steps, he noted through the living room picture window that today was destined to be another stormy and gray day. He longed for a glorious spring morning. The sort where the sun spilled its vibrant colors across the sky. He enjoyed riding Rio on those days, taking in the beauty of the ranch and thanking God for his blessings.

There would be no riding Rio today. He wasn't even going to take time for a cup of coffee. The caffeine would only enhance his already frazzled nerves.

"Going somewhere?" Seth demanded. He had taken the second half of the night watch and now stood in front of the picture window eating a sandwich. He took another bite and eyed Eric with curiosity.

"Yes," Eric answered simply.

Seth's brow furrowed in confusion. "Want me to join you?" He popped the last bite into his mouth, as if proving he was ready for action.

Eric shook his head. "No, thanks. I just texted Cassie. She should be down in a minute."

"She's right down the hall from you, and you texted her?"

"Didn't want to wake Mom and Dad up by pounding on her door," Eric explained.

"You'd rather take her than me?" Seth asked with a knowing smile.

Not willing to buy into his brother's teasing so early in the morning, he simply shook his head. "I need you here to watch the fort and you know it. I assume nothing exciting happened overnight?"

"Nothing out of the ordinary," Seth said. "I even went outside to patrol the perimeter a few times."

Eric didn't like the idea of Seth wandering around outside on his own, but Seth wasn't just his kid brother anymore. He was a trained military veteran, and Eric knew Seth could take care of himself.

"Thanks." Eric clapped him on the shoulder. "I appreciate it."

Cassie appeared then, dressed in jeans and a plain long-sleeved white T-shirt. She looked wide-awake, though he knew he'd disrupted her sleep less than five minutes before. She quickly and quietly traversed the staircase, joining the brothers in the living room.

"What's going on?" she demanded. Her gaze bounced from one brother to the other.

His text had simply asked her to meet him downstairs ASAP.

"Eric was just about to tell us," Seth said.

Eric dragged a hand through his already tousled hair. His thoughts had been swirling for hours. He had replayed the conversation with Frankie over and over, hoping to unearth a clue he had missed. Then his mind would loop around to Lorelei. It was hard to think of her without picturing her lifeless body. He forced his mind to go further back in time, searching for any snippet of conversation they'd had that may offer a clue as to where she would have hidden the evidence.

He didn't think it was on the ranch. For one, it seemed too obvious. For another, he simply didn't think she'd had time. She'd dropped Wyatt off and then had bolted. He was sure after her escape out the bathroom window she hadn't lingered, not even long enough to hide anything, because she had been desperate to get away.

"Uh, Eric," Seth said. "We're still waiting. Where are you headed this time of morning?"

Eric frowned. "I think I might know where Lorelei hid the evidence."

"What?" Seth said the same moment Cassie demanded, "Where?"

"I'm not positive. It's a long shot, but there's this abandoned church out on Old Crossing Trail."

Seth nodded contemplatively. "Yeah. I know that place. We used to go on trail rides up that way. If I recall, the structure is in pretty bad shape."

Eric nodded. "It is. But Lorelei and I rode up there one day, and she was curious. We went inside. Anyhow, I think that might be the place."

"Why?" Seth asked.

Cassie looked at him expectantly.

But he didn't want to get into the reasoning with them. Not right now.

"Look, I have no idea if I'm right or not. It's just a hunch. I could be flat-out wrong."

The truth was, it was the only place that had come to mind. And while he had his doubts, it would be ridiculous to not at least check it out. He couldn't ignore the desperate need to do *something*.

"Should we let Detective Bianchi know?" Cassie asked.

Eric glanced at his watch. It wasn't quite six yet. The detective may be up, or he may not be. Eric suspected being a detective called for long hours and a lot of late nights.

"I don't want to call this early. I was thinking we could go up there, check it out ourselves. That way if I'm wrong, we haven't wasted anyone's time." He glanced at Cassie. "Well, I might be wasting your time."

"Chasing down a lead is never a waste of time," Cassie stated. "What are we waiting for?"

That was all the prompting Eric needed to hustle out the door.

Cassie let Eric drive, simply because he knew exactly where they were going and she did not. She wasn't familiar with the old church. Despite her lack of sleep, she was wide-awake. Wired, even.

It was the same feeling she had every time she got close to solving a case.

Seth was still on guard, and they had let the deputy at the end of the driveway know where they were running on a quick errand. Cassie couldn't help but keep a lookout over her shoulder, periodically checking to be sure they weren't being followed. Hopefully it was too early in the morning for their attackers to think about trying to tail them.

The morning was still dark and gray as storm clouds rolled across the sky. Cassie wondered if today would finally be the day that this would all come to an end.

"You're being awfully quiet." She glanced over at

Eric. He was gripping the steering wheel and staring straight ahead as he drove farther into a wooded area.

"This is a long shot. I'm going off a hazy, faded memory. Frankly, I'm worried I'm wrong." Eric slid a quick glance her way, then went back to looking at the road. "If this isn't the place…"

"If this isn't the place," Cassie said calmly, "then you'll keep thinking on it. Detective Bianchi and I will keep digging. We already know far more than we knew before." She paused. "What did you remember?"

For a moment she thought he wasn't going to answer.

Finally, he said, "When Frankie told me Lorelei hid the evidence where she hoped she found her forever, or something like that, I thought she was speaking metaphorically. I thought that could be anywhere in Mulberry Creek. She told me several times how much she loved this town."

"But…?" Cassie knew Eric well enough to understand that was where he was going with the conversation.

"*But*," he agreed, "early this morning as I was tossing and turning, and praying and trying to remember… it came to me. We had taken the horses out for an afternoon ride. We happened across the church. I'd been by it countless times before. Never had it occurred to me to try to go inside. Yet she took one look and was fascinated by the place. I'm not sure it was a great decision, but we tried the lock—it was broken—and we were able to go right in." He scoffed. "I still can't believe we didn't fall through the floor. And that was years ago. I can't imagine what shape this place is in now."

"You think that's where the evidence is?"

He nodded. "I remember her saying something when we were looking around." He shrugged. "We'd been dating awhile by then. She took my hands and said she hoped she found her forever with me." He let out a wry laugh. "Less than a week later, she took off. I guess I blocked the memory from my mind because it seemed like—"

"Eric!" Cassie excitedly slapped the dashboard. "That has to be it. This has to be the place. I'm sure that's what she meant."

While Eric didn't look convinced, Cassie's heart beat out a chaotic rhythm. She understood he was probably afraid to hope, afraid of disappointment. Yet Cassie didn't believe for one second that Lorelei's words were a coincidence.

Even though no vehicles were in sight, he flipped the blinker on, then turned off the barely maintained gravel road. The short path leading into the woods seemed to be little more than a trail. It was rutted, with overgrown trees edging in on the path. Cassie tried not to think of what all those branches were doing to her paint job.

If this was the place, and she highly suspected it was, then a bit of scratched paint would be a small price to pay.

"I really hope this pans out, because I've come up with nothing else."

Cassie looked around, taking in the overgrown area. The church was almost decrepit. The windows broken, the roof sagging. The old gray wood weathered and probably rotting. It was surrounded by a field of knee-high grass and weeds. Trees encircled the perimeter. Yet it was lovely, in a heartbreaking way. Cassie couldn't help but wonder what had happened to the congregation to make them fade away. Had they simply started going to the bigger churches as the town of Mulberry Creek had started to grow? She would never know.

"Cassie," Eric said, his voice almost a low hum of warning.

It sent tingles up her spine. And not the good kind. She whipped around in her seat, expecting to find that they had been followed after all.

She saw nothing, but every cell in her body was on high alert anyway.

"Not behind us." Eric's tone was still quiet, almost anxious, as he stopped the vehicle. "In front of us."

Her heart hammered as she wondered how someone had gotten ahead of them. Had someone figured out the location before Eric had?

She realized he was pointing, and as the breeze fluttered, something crimson caught her eye. A piece of fabric waving from a tree.

Before she could ask what it was, Eric slid from the Cherokee. She tossed the door open and hurried after him. He closed the distance in long, quick strides, and then they were standing in front of a red scarf, carefully looped around a tree branch in a way that could not be accidental. The scarf hadn't been picked up by the wind and deposited here. This had been intentional.

Despite looking a bit bedraggled, it was clearly out of place here. Something new in this place that was very, very old.

"It's Lorelei's," Eric said, calmly, though Cassie knew his emotions had to be tumultuous. He ran his hand over the fabric, slightly tattered due to the wind, but not faded, indicating it hadn't been here long.

"Are you sure?" Cassie asked, though under the circumstances, she couldn't imagine anyone else would have left it.

"Positive." He let his hand fall. "She was wearing it the night she dropped Wyatt off. It matched her lipstick."

The lipstick she used to write the cryptic message on the mirror.

"She wanted someone to know she'd been here," Cassie said appreciatively. "If we had any doubt this was the place before, this scarf proves you were right."

"She knew I come this way a lot," Eric admitted. "Up and down this stretch is my favorite place to ride Rio. The field behind the church is the perfect open place for him to run. From there, the scarlet scarf would be hard to miss. She must've known I'd find it eventually."

The wind picked up, rustling the leaves and wrapping Cassie in an icy embrace. It was also chilling to know that this was one of the last places Lorelei had visited while alive. How long after she left here had she been killed?

Not long.

The scarf snapped in the wind, as if urging them to get moving.

She couldn't help but think of how scared Lorelei must have been, coming out here all alone. Knowing someone wanted her dead. Had she felt as if she was being stalked? Had she been terrified? Or had she just done what she thought she needed to do, not knowing she'd be breathing her last breath so soon?

Cassie shuddered.

Eric grabbed her elbow and pulled her toward him.

"Let's get inside. Now that we're here, I just want to get this over with."

Together they trudged through the tall dew-damp grass.

"Be careful." Eric tapped the wood with his boot. "I don't know how sturdy the staircase is."

They gingerly climbed the steps, ending up on the small platform that led into the church. Cassie couldn't help but look over her shoulder one more time. The feeling of being followed felt ingrained after this past week.

No one was there. She chided herself for letting her nerves get the better of her.

Eric tugged on the door. The hinges creaked painfully as the door slowly crept inward. They were hit by a musty scent.

"Watch your step," Eric said. "Or maybe I should go in, and you can wait outside. I don't know how safe it is."

"I'm going with you," Cassie said, her tone warning him not to argue. This had to be a difficult time for him. She'd been with him this far and wasn't going to abandon him now.

They stepped inside, Eric going first. He tested the wooden planked floor and deemed it safe.

It was a small church. The narthex was closed off from the sanctuary by a set of swinging doors. An alcove with coatracks was to the left, and a staircase to the right led down to what Cassie assumed was a basement.

"This way, I suppose." He moved straight ahead. He gingerly pushed one of the swinging doors open. Cassie wouldn't have been surprised if it had toppled right out of the door frame.

She looked around the sanctuary. The pews had been pulled out. Some of the windows were boarded, and some were wide-open. Cassie wondered if they'd been filled with stained glass at one time. Here, too, the floor looked questionable, but after a few steps, she decided it seemed sturdy enough.

"I think over there it's rotted." Eric pointed to a large, discolored spot off to the left. Then upward. "The ceiling has clearly been leaking for years. Maybe even decades, for all I know. We'll need to stay clear of that area."

Cassie glanced around. There wasn't much to see. The inside of the church had been stripped bare. If she'd been hoping for a box of clues wrapped in a bright red ribbon to match the bright red scarf, she'd have been disappointed.

Cassie looked to Eric, wondering if he had any answers. His gaze scoured the room. His brow furrowed, as if he was deep in thought.

It was difficult to not interrupt him, demand to know what he was thinking, but she crossed her arms over her chest to try to restrain her curiosity.

She waited.

And waited.

They had come this far and this had to be the place. So where could the evidence be?

Eric turned and began to carefully make his way toward the altar. Not knowing if the rest of the floor was stable, Cassie stayed where she was.

"We were standing right here, in front of the altar, when she said it."

I hope I've found my forever. With you.

Cassie heard the wind gusting outside and wondered

if it was going to storm soon. She hoped they were out of the church before long.

Please, Lord, I know You led us here. Please show us what we came to find.

Eric knelt down and studied the floor. His hand rested on a spot in front of him.

"What is it?" Cassie took a step toward him. The floor groaned ominously.

"You better stay where you are. Just in case the floor won't hold us both." He looked down, then back at her again. "There's a crimson *X* on this floorboard. It's Lorelei's lipstick. I'm sure of it."

Thank you, Lorelei, Cassie thought in admiration. Her life had been on the line, yet she'd had the where-withal to leave clues behind.

"I can tell that the floor has been pried up." Eric tried wedging his fingers under the floorboard. "There are fresh splinters in the wood that don't match the weathered grain."

Cassie's heart skipped a beat. This was it. She had no doubt now. They were about to uncover the evidence that could change everything.

Eric continued to try easing the wood up with his fingers. He glanced at her. Frustration etched across his face. "It won't budge. It's like she pried it out, then hammered it back in place."

"Eric, I think this will help." She pulled her Swiss Army knife out of her jacket pocket. Bending over, she slid it across the floor to him.

A whisper of a smile crossed his face. "Always prepared, aren't you?"

She shrugged. "It's all part of the job."

Only this wasn't a job. Not anymore. Not even close.

This had become personal in a way she never could have imagined. The depth of her feelings for Eric scared her. Though he said he wanted to explore a relationship, she just didn't know if she could give her heart to him. If it didn't work out, losing him a second time could destroy what was left of her tattered heart.

Using the blade of the knife, Eric carefully pried at the wood. Once the blade provided some leverage, the wooden floor plank popped right up. Eric's eyes widened, and he blew out a breath.

"Eric, is it there?" she demanded, part of her already knowing the answer. She fought the urge to run to him.

"It's here." He reached down and pulled out a large manila envelope.

Outside the wind gusted, thunder rumbled and the distinct cadence of rain began to beat against the roof. Lightning flickered through the damaged windows. Heavy rivulets of rain began to stream through the roof, spilling out onto the floor in the place that Eric had warned her was rotting.

They couldn't stay here. The longer they were here, the more dangerous Cassie realized this church was. It was only by the grace of God they hadn't fallen through the floor yet. Thunder rumbled again, and the entire structure seemed to shake, setting Cassie's nerves on edge. She couldn't help but imagine an enormous gust of wind could topple the church right over. She was suddenly nervous, and her heartbeat sped up.

"We should go. This storm sounds like it's picking up in intensity. I don't want to be caught here if things get bad."

Eric stood clutching the envelope. She could tell he wanted to open it.

"According to Frankie, this should hold everything we need to know," Eric said. "It should be enough to put Tom McClellan away."

"Let's bring everything to Detective Bianchi," Cassie urged. "He'll know where to go from here."

"I don't know if I can wait that long."

"Let's at least wait until we get in the vehicle. The longer we stay here, the more convinced I am that the floor is about to give way."

Eric nodded and carefully moved toward her. The boards creaked and groaned their protest. Cassie thought the floor looked like it was sagging under his weight, but perhaps it was just a trick of shadows.

"I want to get home to Wyatt. Thank you for coming with me."

"Of course. We're in this together, remember?"

He slid a serious look her way. "We are, aren't we?"

Holding the envelope in one hand, he pushed open the crooked swinging door with the other. Thunder boomed outside. Cassie jumped, so startled at first that she didn't notice the woman in the entryway smiling at them.

She blinked, did a double take and felt her heartbeat ratchet up to an alarming degree.

"I knew I could count on the two of you to find what I've been looking for." Frankie raised a pistol and slowly arced it back and forth between Cassie and Eric. "Now that I no longer need you, I can *finally* kill you."

THIRTEEN

Trepidation, cold and icy, trickled down Eric's spine as he took in the sight of the woman pointing a gun at him and the woman that he loved. There was no denying it. He loved Cassie. He'd loved her to some degree most of his life. First as a friend, then as more. Even when he'd been angry with her, part of him had known he was in the wrong, and he still cared for her.

"Frankie," he said, his tone full of disgust, "somehow I'm not even surprised to see you." A niggling little voice in his head had warned he shouldn't trust the woman.

"You can call me Francesca. Frankie was an awful nickname my sister came up with. I always hated it."

Francesca, he thought, was somehow more fitting.

"How did you find us here?" Cassie demanded.

"Of all the questions you could ask, that's what you want to know?" Francesca asked with an amused smile. "The answer is easy enough. Before Roger threw the Molotov cocktail through the cabin window, he placed a tracking device on your vehicle."

A tracking device. That would explain it. In all the chaos it had never occurred to Cassie, or Eric either, that the man who started the fire had been there for anything other than just that.

"Roger?" Cassie asked. "The bald man? The one who shot at us in town, pushed us into a river and then set fire to Eric's parents' home?"

"One and the same," Francesca confirmed. "He and that nitwit Dax made it clear they couldn't get the job done. So, my father sent me. I don't mess around, as you are about to find out."

As Eric listened, he tried to discreetly slide between Cassie and the aim of Francesca's gun. Maybe he could shove Cassie back, behind the swinging doors. If he did that, she could run through the sanctuary, crawl through one of the broken windows and get help.

"I don't think so." Francesca immediately noted what he was trying to do. "Both of you, where I can see you. Cassie, I know you're armed. Pull your gun out slowly, then slide it over here. Don't even think about shooting me because, I promise you, I will shoot him first." She flashed them a smug smile. "When I told you I never shot a gun before, I lied. I'm quite good at it."

"Shooting a gun? Or lying?" Eric asked, hoping to buy some time.

"I have quite a talent for both, actually." Francesca looked quite pleased with herself. "Now come on, Cassie. Hand it over."

Eric wanted to tell Cassie to take the shot, but he could hardly say that out loud. She knelt down and slid the gun across the floor. It landed several feet away from Francesca. The woman looked annoyed that she had to retrieve it. She did so without taking her eyes off them.

Eric's mind went to the Swiss Army knife he'd used

to pry up the floor. He had slid it into his back pocket when he was done with it. There was no way he could reach for it, not under Francesca's watchful eye.

"Everything you told us was a lie?" Cassie demanded.

"No. Almost everything I told you was the truth. Our father is a very wealthy, very accomplished criminal. My sister did discover his proclivity for illegal activity and disagreed with it. She was compiling evidence, as you see." She nodded toward the envelope in Eric's hand. "Because of that, she had to be silenced."

"Didn't *Regina* mean anything to you?" Eric asked.

Francesca looked momentarily startled.

"I told you Detective Bianchi was good," Cassie said. "Don't look so surprised that he figured you out. Francesca and Regina McClellan. Your father is Tom McClellan from Seattle. That's where you and your sister grew up, right? It's where your father still lives and runs his illegal arms business."

"Your detective determined that from *Aunt Frankie*?" she grated out. For the first time, she looked a little off-kilter. Clearly she hadn't expected to be found out. She had given them too few details and had thought herself far too clever.

"Wyatt helped us out," Eric said. "He remembered you called his mom Gina. Gina and Frankie. Regina and Francesca." Eric shrugged. "The names were enough to get the detective started. When Wyatt said his mom lived by a needle when she was a child, well, that really helped a lot."

"Wyatt, that little rascal." Francesca's tone held equal parts adoration and frustration. "He gave me away. But it isn't his fault. You were never supposed to catch us the day I took him from the ranch. The deputy guarding your driveway was a hard one to shake. I wasted precious minutes trying to convince him I was harmless before I was able to make my move. Then I had to change out of the frumpy church dress and into that ridiculous uniform. It all took far too long. Of course, when I realized you were behind me, I knew I would never be able to outrun you. I had to think quick on my feet, just like I always do. It was up to me to come up with a backup plan. I called my father's minion, Roger, and told him I was being followed. I let him know what I needed him to do. Only it took him *forever* to get to the cabin. When he did, he provided the distraction I needed to get away."

"You had your henchman set a cabin on fire with your nephew inside," Eric growled. "Wyatt could have been seriously hurt. Or worse."

She scoffed. "I knew you would never let that happen. And I was right, wasn't I?"

"There were so many ways that plan could have gone sideways," Eric said.

"But it didn't," Francesca stated. "My plans rarely do. Getting caught taking Wyatt from the ranch was a rare, unfortunate exception."

"What you're saying is that you're complicit in all of this," Cassie pointed out. "Detective Bianchi knows who you are. You aren't going to get away with this."

Francesca frowned but didn't seem too alarmed. "I suppose we'll just have to leave the country. Move somewhere with no extradition treaty. The Maldives and Morocco are both quite lovely." She shrugged, as if it was no big deal to pick up her life and move to a new continent.

Eric got the impression that Francesca, and probably

her father, had already given the matter some thought. Under the circumstances, it wouldn't be all that surprising.

"What was your part in all of this?" He was already pretty sure he knew.

"Am I going to have to spell it all out for you?" she sneered.

"Afraid so, because I just can't wrap my head around a situation this warped."

"I am my father's daughter," Francesca stated, a note of arrogance tingeing her tone, "and unlike Regina, I've always been proud of it."

A rumble of thunder shook the church, vibrating the floor beneath their feet. Eric realized then that it was because of the storm that they hadn't heard this woman's approach. The ranch was miles away, and if she shot them, would it be mistaken for a clap of thunder, if the gunshot was heard at all?

"Our father sacrificed for us," Francesca said. "He went to great lengths to be sure we had the best of everything. But was my sister grateful? No. No, she was not. She turned on him. That means she turned on me, too. Oh, I tried to convince her I was on her side. I tried to get close, make her believe I wanted what she wanted." Francesca frowned. "But she was so cynical. No matter what I did, what I said, I couldn't get her to trust me completely."

"I'm sure she suspected you were only trying to get close to her to steal her evidence," Cassie said. "Good for her for not buying into your lies."

"No," Francesca snapped. "There was nothing good about her. Regina turned on her family. She had no gratitude whatsoever. My sister was determined to keep Wyatt from us. It took me years to convince her that I had come to her way of thinking. I spent time with her in Florida. I doted on Wyatt. I did my best to make her think I'd walked away from our father, just as she had. Only she never really believed me."

"Who killed her?" A chill crept up Eric's spine because he suspected he knew the answer.

"I did," Francesca stated with ease.

"You killed your own sister?" Eric asked in disgust. "What kind of monster are you?"

For the first time, Francesca's cool demeanor slipped. "Do *not* blame me. Regina brought this on herself. She had ample warning. Father gave her multiple chances to let this nasty situation drop. So what if she didn't like what he did? She didn't have to be a part of it. All she had to do was stay out of it. It's not our fault she refused to do that."

"You worked to gain her trust. Then you double-crossed her," Eric accused.

Francesca shrugged. "When she went missing from Florida, it was easy to guess where she'd gone. I tracked her down here. By the time I arrived, she'd already dropped Wyatt off with you. I was able to find her using her new identity, Vanessa Walters."

Vanessa Walters. The name clicked in Eric's mind immediately. They had assumed that it was an identity that Francesca had stolen, when really, it was simply the new name that Regina, Lorelei, had been using.

"She had rented a vehicle and the cabin," Francesca said.

"Is that where you killed her?" Eric asked.

"Yes. Her planning gave me a place to stay and a vehicle to use. One that couldn't be tied to me. Until you spotted me leaving the ranch and ruined it all. But thanks to Roger, the place has burned to the ground. It would be impossible to prove that my sister or I was ever there."

Eric shuddered at the realization that his son had been taken to the same place his mother had been murdered.

"You see," she continued, "I was able to retrieve the original packet of evidence. I found it in the cabin while she was off dispensing Wyatt with you. I burned it in the fireplace. I knew I had to dispose of her. There was really no other option. Regina was irredeemable. Untrustworthy. But she told me killing her wouldn't make a difference because she'd made a duplicate of everything. She gave me a hint about where she left it."

"Why would she do that?" Cassie wondered. "She had to have known it would put Eric in danger."

"Oh, I don't think she meant to admit to that." Francesca waved the gun around dismissively. "She was groggy, just about to slip under, when she said it."

"You drugged her," Cassie stated. "There were traces of Rohypnol in her system. That's how you overpowered her and strangled her."

"She wasn't surprised to see me at the cabin," Francesca admitted. "I told her we needed to sit down and have a heart-to-heart. It was a dreary night. I'd made hot cocoa, with mint, her favorite. A little bit of the drug and a few sips of her drink was all it took to make her defenseless."

Eric let out a disgusted growl of contempt.

"It was a good plan," Francesca said. "Dax was supposed to dispose of the body. He got lazy and tossed her in the river, where she was found far too quickly."

Eric had thought it would be difficult to get the truth out of Francesca, but her hatred for her sister combined with her pride made for a woman who was ready to spill all with no provocation.

"How does Wyatt fit into this?" Eric demanded. She had kidnapped him, claiming it was to keep him safe from her father's henchmen, but Eric knew better.

"Wyatt is our legacy. Father is so anxious to meet him. I'll take him, raise him as my own."

"Over my dead body," Eric grated out.

Francesca laughed. "Precisely. At least we're on the same page about that, because I do plan to kill you. I did all of this to preserve my father's dynasty. I did it so that one day I could inherit his empire. Wyatt belongs with us. He's a McClellan, and Father will be pleased that I'm returning him to the fold. Raising him as my child, making him the future heir, will just be the frosting on the proverbial cupcake. I've always wanted a child of my own. Now I don't have to go through any messy entanglements to get one."

Eric's ire sizzled through him. She spoke of Wyatt as if he were a mere possession.

"You are evil." He stared Francesca down, hoping the woman would keep her attention, her gun, trained on him. He'd gotten Cassie into this mess. He desperately wanted to get her out of it. If he rushed Francesca, he risked getting shot. But if he didn't—

Cassie's leg swung out in a perfectly executed round-house kick before he had the chance to finish that thought.

Francesca screamed, either in surprise or pain or both, as Cassie's foot connected forcefully with her chest. She'd been distracted, so Cassie had taken her chance.

Francesca's gun went flying as she stumbled backward. Her arms windmilled, her feet flailed and then she tumbled, her backside hitting the floor hard. She landed in a puddle, the place where the rain had been sneaking in through the roof for years.

The double swinging doors flew open.

"Police!"

Detective Bianchi and a uniformed officer burst into the room, guns drawn, ready for action.

Cassie had never been so happy to see anyone in her life. She'd been waiting for just the right moment to attack, knowing it was risky, and she could be shot in the process, but according to Francesca, she was going to die anyway. She'd rather die fighting than just give up.

With a soft crunch, the rotting wood gave way. Francesca screamed again, her hands frantically grabbing, catching nothing but the edges of the rotting floor as it crumbled, and she tumbled to the ground under the church.

For a moment, there was silence.

Then the woman moaned. A low, miserable, guttural sound.

The detective lowered his gun and raised his eyebrows at Eric and Cassie.

"Are you two all right?"

"Yes," Cassie said.

The other officer pulled a flashlight from his utility belt and shone it down into the hole.

Cassie and Eric leaned forward as well, careful to stay away from the rotting edge. Francesca's leg was clearly broken, and she glared up at them, her face masked in pain and fury. She tried to sit, groaned and flopped back down.

"I think I saw steps leading downstairs. I'll administer aid." The officer headed out of the sanctuary.

"Is that Francesca McClellan?" Detective Bianchi questioned.

"Yes," Cassie affirmed. "It's Francesca."

Eric wondered, "How did you—"

"Your brother called me." The detective frowned as he holstered his gun. "He told me what you were up to and that you didn't want to waste my time with it in case it didn't pan out. You should've let me be the judge of that."

"She killed Lorelei," Eric said, still unable to think of her as Regina. "She killed her own sister. I'm having a hard time comprehending that level of evil. I would have done almost anything to keep my own sister alive."

"That's because you're a decent human being," Detective Bianchi stated. "And not a coldhearted, greedy, callous monster."

That about summed up what Cassie was thinking. To her, to Eric, family was everything. It took a special kind of awful to do the things Francesca had done.

"That took guts, Cassie," Eric said in appreciation.

She shook her head. "Not really. She was going to kill us. She made that clear. I saw a chance, and I took it."

"Looks like we were just a few seconds late," Detective Bianchi said. "We were about to storm the sanctuary when we heard her scream."

"Can we go back to the ranch?" Eric asked. "I really need to see my son."

Detective Bianchi hesitated a moment. "I have a lot of questions for you, both of you, but I know where to find you. As soon as I saw the white SUV, I called in backup. They should be here any minute, including an ambulance. Go ahead and head out. I'll come to the ranch as soon as everything is wrapped up here."

Eric held up the manila envelope, then handed it to the detective. "I haven't had a chance to look inside, but I suspect this might help answer the questions we all have."

When Detective Bianchi finally showed up at the house, the day was nearly over. The first thing he told Eric and Cassie was that Francesca had been charged with a multitude of crimes, ranging from the murder of Regina McClellan to impersonating an officer.

"If there's any justice in this world, and I believe there is," Detective Bianchi said, "then Francesca McClellan will be locked up for a very, very long time."

"What about Tom McClellan?" Cassie asked.

"Authorities in Seattle are on their way to arrest him as we speak."

With that knowledge, Eric felt as if he and his son were finally safe.

They were seated around the kitchen table. The detective was nearly ready to take their statements, but he wanted to get them up-to-date first.

"I have more good news. When we told Dax Donaldson that Francesca implicated him in her sister's murder, he decided to talk. He said the man whom he only knew as 'the Boss' told him he needed to help out a woman at a remote cabin. He claimed he didn't realize until he got there what he was helping her with. He's about ready to sign a plea deal and will testify that Francesca confessed to him that she strangled the woman, though he had no idea it was her sister. Furthermore, he told us Roger Miller from Kalamazoo is his accomplice, and he was taken into custody less than an hour ago."

"You've had a busy day," Eric said.

The detective nodded. "I feel like I've been running my tail off since the sun came up. But it was worth it. This case was blown wide open today."

"I've been praying for this outcome," Cassie said.

"God has answered your prayers," Detective Bianchi replied. "I've looked over the evidence in the envelope. We have pages of financial records, phone records, sales records. A flash drive with hours of phone calls. I haven't listened to all of them, but the few I did were incriminating."

"So that's it?" Eric asked. "They'll all be going to prison?"

"It sure looks that way. Even if both Dax and Roger get plea deals, they'll still be spending some time behind bars," Detective Bianchi said. "Now, I came here to get your statements. I'd like to get started on that."

They spoke to the detective at great length, describing the day's events, beginning with the memory Eric had that triggered the trip to the church. By the time the detective was done questioning them, they were both physically and mentally drained.

When the front door closed behind him, Cassie turned to Eric. "I should be going, too."

Her words startled him, though he realized they shouldn't have.

"I'll be safe in my own home now. Everyone is behind bars. You got the answers you were looking for. You don't need me anymore."

That wasn't true. He felt as though he needed Cassie more than ever. He knew he needed to make her understand that.

"Eric, Wyatt's asking for you," his mother said from the top of the stairs. "He wants you to read him a book and tuck him in."

Cassie placed her hand on his arm. "You should go. He needs to know you're here for him."

Eric was torn. His son needed him, but maybe Cassie did as well. "Cass—"

"Daddy?"

Eric glanced up at the staircase. Wyatt now stood next to his grandma. He looked adorable, yet so young and vulnerable, in his pajamas, holding his bear close. "I want a story."

"Go," Cassie urged.

So, he did.

By the time he came downstairs, Cassie was gone.

FOURTEEN

The next morning Cassie sat in her home office, scrolling through emails she had been neglecting while trying to help Eric. Though her landlord had taken care of the repairs to her office downtown, she wasn't quite ready to operate there yet. There was plenty she could do from home. She had several inquiries and was trying to determine which cases would be the best fit. She needed to get to work. Staying busy would keep her mind off Eric.

Off his family, his precious son.

Her heart ached. A constant pang that would not subside.

She missed her mom. Though she and her birth mother were slowly building a bond, they still barely knew each other. And she lived so far away. Her brothers, too. Cassie had always wanted a family that was close. Not in physicality, but in heart. She longed for the organized chaos of the ranch. The big family dinners, the endless conversations, the constant love and support.

As she listlessly scrolled through another message, she realized she was lonely.

Obviously Eric had wanted to talk last night. She suspected he would ask if they could give a relationship a try. But the thought terrified her. She'd hurriedly packed her bags and raced out the door. Maybe she was a coward, but she couldn't bear to have her heart broken by him again.

The problem was that she didn't just love Eric. She loved his whole family and already adored his son. If a relationship between them didn't work out, she didn't think she could stand losing the whole family all over again.

Her cell phone rang. She grabbed it, irritated with herself that she hoped it was him. It wasn't. It was Danae, her birth mother. To her surprise, she was comforted the moment she saw Danae's name.

Perhaps she had begun to depend on the woman more than she realized.

"Hey, there," Cassie said, by way of greeting.

"Hey, yourself," Danae said lightly. "I haven't heard from you in a while. I've been thinking about you, and I know you're probably working, but I just felt such a strong desire to call you right now."

Cassie glanced Heavenward, knowing what Danae felt was a nudge from God, just when Cassie needed her the most.

"How are you doing?" Danae asked.

Cassie pinched the bridge of her nose. To her horror, her voice crackled with unshed tears. "It's been a crazy week."

Danae's tone was gentle, hopeful, when she asked, "Do you want to tell me about it? I've been told I'm a good listener."

"Yes." Cassie relaxed, sinking back in her chair. "I think I'd like that a lot."

Her words began pouring out, confiding everything

to Danae. Not only the frightening aspects of the week, but she told Danae about Eric as well.

She hadn't planned on delving into their history, but Danae *was* a good listener. It was obvious she longed to know more about Cassie, about her life. Cassie found herself sharing everything.

Danae had become a Christian after meeting and marrying her husband, Ron. When Cassie was done baring her soul, Danae said, "Maybe it's time to let go and let God."

Cassie was silent a moment, allowing the words to sink in.

"That's what I had to do," Danae said. "I had to let go of the hurts and anger of the past. I had to let go of everything that was dragging me down. I was angry at myself for giving you away. I was angry at my parents for not supporting me. When I met Ron, he led me to Jesus. I remember a verse that I felt the pastor shared just for me. He said, *Let all bitterness, and wrath, and anger, and clamour, and evil speaking, be put away from you, with all malice: And be ye kind one to another, tenderhearted, forgiving one another, even as God for Christ's sake hath forgiven you.*" She released a shuddering breath. "I knew then it was time to forgive not only my parents, but myself."

By the time Cassie got off the phone, she felt a little more lighthearted. And a whole lot more connected to her birth mother. Danae was right. It was time for Cassie to let go of all of the hurts. She needed to forgive Maggie Anderson for her betrayal. She needed to forgive Eric for his hurtful words.

It was time to let go of the past.

She had no sooner put the phone down than the doorbell rang. She instinctively knew it was Eric. Contradictory emotions swirled through her. She was nervous, afraid of where the impending conversation would lead. Yet she was joyful as well, her heart swelling at the realization that Eric wasn't willing to just let her walk away.

When she opened the door and found him there, he simply said, "I've missed you."

"I haven't even been gone a day. Here I thought you'd be happy to be rid of me," she said lightly.

He shook his head. "Never. I don't mean I just missed you since yesterday. A part of me has been missing you for six years."

It was a gorgeous morning, finally free of the rain clouds that had been plaguing them all week. Molten-gold sunshine spilled across the sky. Cassie stepped onto her front porch. After closing the door behind her, she took a seat on the porch swing.

Eric sat next to her.

Her heart swelled with the love she'd been trying to ignore.

Cassie's eyes widened when she heard the plaintive meow. Eric had placed the cat carrier by the porch swing, out of the way where she hadn't immediately spotted it.

"Is that why you stopped by? Did you bring me the kitten?" She leaned around him, trying to peer inside. "Your timing is perfect. I could really use the company."

"Part of the reason," Eric admitted. He had kitten supplies for her in the truck, but he would grab them later. "I thought you might be lonely here all by yourself." He leaned over, opened the carrier and pulled out Cuddles.

"It's funny how well you still know me." She accepted the kitten, who immediately began to purr. Eric thought maybe those internet articles were onto something. Purring did seem to bring instant peace. At least to Cassie.

He wanted to ask her about her comment. Press the matter and tell her there was no reason for her to be lonely. She was welcome at the ranch at any time. More than welcome. He longed to have her there. His whole family did.

Before he could get those words out, she spoke again.

"How is Wyatt this morning?"

"He asked about you before he even had his breakfast," Eric admitted, grateful that she had asked and even more grateful for the genuine concern in her eyes. "He was pretty disappointed when I explained to him that you have your own house and that you don't actually live at the ranch. He's hoping you'll come visit soon."

Cassie dipped her head, and he wished he knew what she was thinking.

"I spoke to Detective Bianchi this morning," he continued, sure that she would want to know. "Tom McClellan was apprehended at the Seattle-Tacoma International Airport, where his private jet was waiting. Flight plans revealed he was headed to Morocco."

Her head snapped up and a look of relief washed over her face. "That's wonderful news. Now hopefully the only place he'll be headed is prison. Francesca, too."

"It's looking likely. Roger Miller," he said, naming the bald accomplice, "wasn't very happy about being taken into custody last night, especially when he found out Dax turned him in. It sounds like he's willing to talk from the get-go."

Cassie nodded. "They're going to turn on each other. That'll be to our advantage. How are your parents doing?"

Their home, their belongings, had been a total loss. His mother, always the epitome of strength, had said she was not going to mourn the loss of Ella's keepsakes. Instead, she would cherish the memories she held in her heart and thank God every day for the family she had left on earth.

"My parents are going to move in with Seth until their house can be rebuilt. I offered to let them stay at my place. Mom feels it would be best for Wyatt and me to be on our own. She said it would be easier to build a strong bond that way. Also, it might be less confusing for Wyatt as he tries to settle into his new life." Eric smiled. "Of course, with them just on the other side of the property, I'm sure she'll be stopping by plenty. Which is just fine with me."

"I can't imagine them staying away. Your family is amazing," Cassie said.

"I'm pretty blessed."

He went into further details of the case, explaining some of the particulars that Detective Bianchi had gone over with him. Cassie listened intently, offering commentary here and there.

He didn't tell Cassie about the note Lorelei had left him in the envelope. She had apologized for keeping Wyatt from him and pleaded for his forgiveness. She claimed she was doing what was best. Eric still thought it would have been best if Lorelei had confided in him right away.

But she hadn't, and there was no changing the past.

He would eventually tell Cassie about the letter, but not today. He wanted today to be all about him and Cassie and the future he hoped they would have.

When he'd come down the stairs last night to find Cassie gone, he'd felt so defeated. So deflated. So... hopeless.

But his mother, always the voice of reason, had asked him a simple question.

"You love her," she began. "I know you do. Are you really willing to let her slip away?"

He realized that, no, he was not willing to let Cassie disappear from his life again.

Eric had been ready to race out the door at that moment, but Julia suggested he wait until morning. Everyone's emotions were running high after the events in the church. As much as he hated the thought of Cassie being alone, she had chosen to go. He realized they all needed some time to mentally decompress.

But once morning came, he'd gone shopping for the kitten, then raced back home to pack her up and head to Cassie's. When Wyatt found out where he was going, he had begged to go along. Only a trip out to the barn with Julia to visit Pumpkin had distracted him.

Eric knew that Wyatt had grown attached to Cassie in a short time. He thought, hoped, Cassie had gotten attached to Wyatt as well. More than attached. He hoped she loved Wyatt, or was starting to. He'd seen flickers of it, adoration, in the way she looked at his son.

Had he seen those flickers of adoration in the way she looked at *him*?

Yeah, he thought he had. Prayed he had.

"Cassie, I know you've had a rough time of it the past

few years. You were never meant to be on your own. But you have been. You've been let down by people the closest to you. Including me. Especially me. I don't ever want you to feel alone again. I want you to know how much you are cherished, how much you are loved. I want to be there for you, to support you."

Her eyes locked with his, and he thought he heard her breath catch.

It would be so easy right now to walk away, to pack up his heart and try to pack up his feelings, but he owed Cassie this. He owed it to both of them to put himself out there and try to right the wrongs of the past.

Please, Lord, help me to say the right thing. Please open her heart to me.

Cassie sat perfectly still. Was Eric going to suggest they be friends again, as he had the day in the barn? Was that where he was going with those wonderful words? The sentiments that were reaching in, grabbing her heart? Or was there more to this?

The serious way he was looking at her made her dare to hope that there was something greater at stake here. He had said she was loved. By him? What kind of love? The kind one friend had for another?

He paused so long she thought her heart would rattle right out of her chest if he didn't say something soon.

"Cassie, I made a terrible mistake all those years ago. The way I treated you, it ate away at me. It was unfair. But I think we've moved past it."

"I said I forgive you," she reminded him. But Eric seemed to be determined to make her understand how sincere he'd been.

"I want more than your forgiveness. You're the most

amazing woman I've ever met. You are strong and fearless. Loving and kind. You are beautiful inside and out. I want you in my life. I don't ever want to let you go again."

She had dreamed of a moment like this.

Despite the hurt of the past, she knew it was time to forgive. It was time to move on.

More than that, it was time to take a leap of faith.

Let go and let God.

Let God lead her into a future unhindered by the past. She claimed to be strong in her Christian faith. But was she really? Not if she clung to her own fears and misgivings.

A verse from Philippians flittered through her mind. It was one that Ella had said often toward the end.

Be careful for nothing; but in every thing by prayer and supplication with thanksgiving let your requests be made known unto God. And the peace of God, which passeth all understanding, shall keep your hearts and minds through Christ Jesus.

If Ella, facing the trials she'd faced in her darkest days, could give it over to God, surely Cassie could as well. Cassie remembered the peace that Ella had felt. Even facing death, Ella had been wrapped in a comfort, in a peace that surpassed all understanding.

Cassie wanted that with all of her heart.

"I've already missed so much time with you," he continued. "And I've missed so much time with my son. If this past week has reminded me of anything, it's that life is too short not to cherish every moment." He paused, his dark brown eyes locking with hers, seeming to see her down to her very soul. "I love you, Cassie Jolie Anderson, and I think you love me, too."

His words seemed to melt away the last of her fears.

"I do. Oh, how I do," she said solemnly. She meant the words with her whole heart.

He nodded. "Then maybe not today, or tomorrow, or even next week, but someday, someday soon…I want you to be my wife." He hesitated, seeming unsure of himself, then pulled a ring box out of his pocket.

Cassie felt her eyes widen, and her hands began to tremble.

That could not possibly be what she thought it was, what she wished it was. She pulled her gaze from the box and met his eyes. The dark brown depths were so familiar to her. She wanted to look into them every day for the rest of her life.

He must've seen the hope she held in her heart, because his trepidation seemed to fade away.

"This was my grandmother's wedding ring. My mom gave it to me last night. She said she couldn't think of anyone she'd rather see wearing it than you." He pulled in a deep breath. "I couldn't agree more."

Her heart seemed to swirl and dance in her chest. All the years of heartache and loneliness began to fade away. Before he even said the words she knew he was about to say, her mind conjured images of a glorious future. The one she'd dreamed of.

Eric.

The ranch and the home she loved because of everything it embodied.

His amazing family.

And now his precious son.

It was a future so blessed, it could only have been created by her Lord.

Let go and let God…and see all of the wonders He has in store for you.

"Cassie, will you marry me?" He flipped open the box, and a lovely antique ring rested inside. The princess-cut diamond glittered in the light of the brilliant morning sunshine.

"Yes," she said breathlessly. "Yes, yes, yes!"

He chuckled. "I was really hoping you would say that."

He pulled the ring from the box and gently slid it onto her finger.

Cassie held out her hand, not only admiring the stone and the ornate setting, but admiring what it represented. Eric's love.

His family's heritage.

She couldn't think of anything he could give her in that moment that would be more meaningful than his grandmother's ring.

"I have Wyatt now," he reminded her. "I'm kind of a package deal these days."

Leaning toward him, Cassie said softly, "I wouldn't have it any other way." Then she kissed him, in case he had any doubts.

EPILOGUE

Six months later...

Cassie stood on the wraparound porch of the ranch house, overlooking the front yard of her home. A party was in full swing. Family, friends and members of their church had come out to celebrate this special day with Cassie and Eric.

Eric's family, including Nina, was all present. Nina had moved back to Mulberry Creek, and she and Cassie had become the best of friends over the summer. Cassie's family was in attendance as well. Her mother and step-father and her brothers had driven from South Dakota for the event.

Over the past several months, Cassie and Danae's bond had grown stronger. On her wedding day, one short month after Eric proposed, Cassie had called Danae *Mom* for the first time. It hadn't been planned. The word simply slipped out. Cassie didn't regret it because it felt right. Danae had cried, but they'd been happy tears.

Since then, she'd spoken with her nearly every day on the phone.

While she still missed the mother who had raised

her, Cassie was so grateful for Danae now, as she began this new phase in her life.

She no longer felt alone, and she was so grateful for the family she had. Even more grateful for the family she and Eric were beginning to create. A week after their wedding, Cassie had formally adopted Wyatt

Her heart was so very full.

She heard the door clatter behind her, and she glanced over her shoulder. Eric came out of the house holding a large, carefully wrapped box.

He grinned at her. "Are you ready for this?"

Her heart swelled at the sight of him She felt so much love for this man.

"I'm ready."

"A present!" Wyatt yelled when he spotted them. He darted away from the group of kids he'd been playing with. Clomping up the steps, he asked, "Is that for me?"

"It's a surprise for all of our guests, including you," Eric said. "Do you want to help us open it?"

Wyatt nodded emphatically.

"We need everyone's attention first."

"Hey, everyone!" Wyatt shouted as he darted back down the steps. "We have a surprise for you!"

Cassie laughed as she carefully followed Eric into the middle of the yard. Barely halfway through her pregnancy, she felt enormous these days, with her swollen ankles and achy back, but she wouldn't have it any other way. She pressed a hand to her stomach, felt the tap of a tiny foot against her palm and was filled with so much happiness she thought she would burst.

"Oh!" Julia crooned from the middle of the crowd. "Is it time for the gender reveal?"

"It's time," Cassie agreed.

Clusters of people, men and women alike who were guests at the baby shower, turned to face Cassie and Eric.

Eric carefully settled the box onto a picnic table.

Nina stood next to Julia. She winked at Cassie. "Am I getting a niece or another nephew? You know I'd be thrilled with either, but I can't handle the suspense."

"Nor can I," Danae said with a laugh.

"Come on now," Julia urged. "I think we've all waited long enough."

"Wyatt, do you think it's a brother or a sister?" James asked.

Cassie and Eric shared a secret smile as Wyatt shrugged while bouncing up and down in excitement.

"Let's find out," Cassie said. "Wyatt, sweetie, can you carefully take the cover off the box?"

Her son nodded, grinned and dutifully pulled the top off the large silver-wrapped box.

As the lid lifted, a blue balloon floated out.

"Another boy!" Seth hooted in delight.

But a moment later, a pink balloon slowly, lazily drifted up alongside the first balloon. Both were anchored to the box, tethered in place by long lengths of ribbon.

The crowd was silent for just a second, and then Julia let out a whoop of joyous surprise.

"Twins!" She clapped a hand to her heart and tears shimmered in her eyes. "A boy and a girl…" she said wistfully.

Eric slid his arm around Cassie's shoulders. "Twins."

The news had come as a surprise to Cassie and Eric when they went in for the ultrasound last week. Up until that point, only one heartbeat had been detected.

The doctor explained sometimes that could happen, depending on how they were positioned.

Yet after the ultrasound, there was no doubt.

"Yes! Two babies!" Wyatt fist-pumped in the air.

"It does run in the family," James said, his tone suspiciously scratchy.

"Ella would be so thrilled." Nina smiled wide, her emotion evident.

Then everyone seemed to rush forward, offering hugs and congratulations.

Cassie could barely contain her joy. This was what she had always wanted. A large, loving, close family. God had answered her prayers in a bigger and better way than she had ever imagined.

She had let go and let God.

In return, He had spilled blessing upon blessing into her life.

She looked Heavenward and whispered a silent *Thank You, Lord.*

* * * * *

If you enjoyed this story, look for these other books by Amity Steffen:

Colorado Ambush
Reunion on the Run

Dear Reader,

Thank you so much for taking the time to be a part of Cassie and Eric's journey. I've had this series in mind for some time, and I couldn't be more excited about finally bringing the Montgomery family into the world. I'm looking forward to continuing with both Seth's and Nina's stories in the near future.

Cassie and Eric both struggle with events from their past. Prior hurts, disappointments and bad choices can be difficult to overcome. But through forgiveness, prayer and learning to give our problems to God, we can prevail, just as Cassie and Eric did.

I love connecting with my readers. For updates on new releases, sales and the occasional giveaway, please join me on Facebook at www.facebook.com/AmitySteffenAuthor.

Blessings to all,
Amity Steffen

UNDERCOVER OPERATION
Pacific Northwest K-9 Unit • by Maggie K. Black

After three bloodhound puppies are stolen, K-9 officer Asher Gilmore and trainer Peyton Burns are forced to go undercover as married drug smugglers to rescue them. But infiltrating the criminals will be more dangerous than expected, putting the operation, the puppies and their own lives at risk.

TRACKED THROUGH THE WOODS
by Laura Scott

Abby Miller is determined to find her missing FBI informant father before the mafia does, but time is running out. Can she trust special agent Wyatt Kane to protect her from the gunmen on her trail, to locate her father—and to uncover an FBI mole?

HUNTED AT CHRISTMAS
Amish Country Justice • by Dana R. Lynn

When single mother Addison Johnson is attacked by a hit man, she learns there's a price on her head. Soon it becomes clear that Isaiah Bender—the bounty hunter hired to track her down for crimes she didn't commit—is her only hope for survival.

SEEKING JUSTICE
by Sharee Stover

With her undercover operation in jeopardy, FBI agent Tiandra Daugherty replaces her injured partner with his identical twin brother, Officer Elijah Kenyon. But saving her mission puts Elijah in danger. Can Tiandra and her K-9 keep him alive before he becomes the next target?

RESCUING THE STOLEN CHILD
by Connie Queen

When Texas Ranger Zane Adcock's grandson is kidnapped and used as leverage to get Zane to investigate an old murder case, he calls his ex-fiancée for help. Zane and retired US marshal Bliss Walker will risk their lives to take down the criminals...and find the missing boy before it's too late.

CHRISTMAS MURDER COVER-UP
by Shannon Redmon

After Detective Liz Burke finds her confidential informant dead and interrupts the killer's escape, she's knocked unconscious and struggles to remember the details of the murder. With a target on her back, she must team up with homicide detective Oz Kelly to unravel a deadly scheme—and stay alive.

Get 3 FREE REWARDS!

We'll send you 2 FREE Books plus a FREE Mystery Gift.

FREE Value Over **$20**

Both the **Love Inspired®** and **Love Inspired®** Suspense series feature compelling novels filled with inspirational romance, faith, forgiveness and hope.

YES! Please send me 2 FREE novels from the Love Inspired or Love Inspired Suspense series and my FREE gift (gift is worth about $10 retail). After receiving them, if I don't wish to receive any more books, I can return the shipping statement marked "cancel." If I don't cancel, I will receive 6 brand-new Love Inspired Larger-Print books or Love Inspired Suspense Larger-Print books every month and be billed just $6.49 each in the U.S. or $6.74 each in Canada. That is a savings of at least 16% off the cover price. It's quite a bargain! Shipping and handling is just 50¢ per book in the U.S. and $1.25 per book in Canada.* I understand that accepting the 2 free books and gift places me under no obligation to buy anything. I can always return a shipment and cancel at any time by calling the number below. The free books and gift are mine to keep no matter what I decide.

Choose one: ☐ **Love Inspired Larger-Print** (122/322 BPA GRPA)   ☐ **Love Inspired Suspense Larger-Print** (107/307 BPA GRPA)   ☐ **Or Try Both!** (122/322 & 107/307 BPA GRRP)

Name (please print)

Address   Apt. #

City   State/Province   Zip/Postal Code

Email: Please check this box ☐ if you would like to receive newsletters and promotional emails from Harlequin Enterprises ULC and its affiliates. You can unsubscribe anytime.

Mail to the Harlequin Reader Service:
IN U.S.A.: P.O. Box 1341, Buffalo, NY 14240-8531
IN CANADA: P.O. Box 603, Fort Erie, Ontario L2A 5X3

Want to try 2 free books from another series? Call 1-800-873-8635 or visit www.ReaderService.com.

*Terms and prices subject to change without notice. Prices do not include sales taxes, which will be charged (if applicable) based on your state or country of residence. Canadian residents will be charged applicable taxes. Offer not valid in Quebec. This offer is limited to one order per household. Books received may not be as shown. Not valid for current subscribers to the Love Inspired or Love Inspired Suspense series. All orders subject to approval. Credit or debit balances in a customer's account(s) may be offset by any other outstanding balance owed by or to the customer. Please allow 4 to 6 weeks for delivery. Offer available while quantities last.

Your Privacy—Your information is being collected by Harlequin Enterprises ULC, operating as Harlequin Reader Service. For a complete summary of the information we collect, how we use this information and to whom it is disclosed, please visit our privacy notice located at corporate.harlequin.com/privacy-notice. From time to time we may also exchange your personal information with reputable third parties. If you wish to opt out of this sharing of your personal information, please visit readerservice.com/consumerschoice or call 1-800-873-8635. **Notice to California Residents**—Under California law, you have specific rights to control and access your data. For more information on these rights and how to exercise them, visit corporate.harlequin.com/california-privacy.

LIRLIS23

HARLEQUIN
PLUS

Try the best multimedia subscription service for romance readers like you!

Read, Watch and Play.

Experience the easiest way to get the romance content you crave.

Start your **FREE TRIAL** at
www.harlequinplus.com/freetrial.